ONLY A DAY AWAY

When Sally is offered a position in New Zealand, she sees it as the opportunity of a lifetime. Unfortunately, her mother doesn't share her view — and neither does her fiancé. Sadly, she hands back his ring and looks to an uncertain future. When Adam arrives in her life though, along with a gorgeous little boy, everything becomes even more complicated. But New Zealand works its own brand of magic, and for Sally an unexpected, whole new life is beginning . . .

CHRISSIE LOVEDAY

◆

ONLY A DAY AWAY

Complete and Unabridged

LINFORD
Leicester

First published in Great Britain in 2008

First Linford Edition
published 2008

British Library CIP Data

Loveday, Chrissie
    Only a day away.—Large print ed.—
Linford romance library
    1. Love stories
    2. Large type books
    I. Title
    823.9'2 [F]

    ISBN 978–1–84782–414–1

Published by
F. A. Thorpe (Publishing)
Anstey, Leicestershire

Set by Words & Graphics Ltd.
Anstey, Leicestershire
Printed and bound in Great Britain by
T. J. International Ltd., Padstow, Cornwall

This book is printed on acid-free paper

Visit the author's website at:
www.chrissieloveday.com

1

'But why New Zealand? You couldn't go much further if you tried.' Sally's mum looked devastated.

'It's only a day away. More or less. And they do have telephones there you know. And a mail service. I can send you letters every day if you really want me to. And photographs.'

'You'll go and find some sheep-farming type and bury yourself in the middle of nowhere forever more. I won't ever get to see my grandchildren.' Her mother was now close to tears. 'Oh Sally, do you have to go? Can't you turn the job down?'

'I could, but I don't want to. And you don't have any grandchildren, not now, not in the foreseeable future.'

'Exactly.'

'And how can you possibly imagine I'd fall for a sheep farmer? What have you got against sheep, anyway?' she asked, trying to lighten the mood. 'Besides, I'm engaged to Rob, aren't I?'

'What does Rob think? He must be devastated.'

Sally frowned. She still had to tackle Rob about her proposed new job.

'He'll understand. It's too good a chance to miss.' She spoke confidently, but she knew that most certainly he would not understand. Nor would he accept her plans without one huge row. But she knew she was doing what was right for her. Their relationship hadn't been working properly for some time. Maybe getting engaged to someone you'd known practically all your life had not been the best of ideas.

They'd been friends from the same street since the same infant school. When he'd shyly asked her to go to see a film with him, aged fourteen, she'd said yes, thinking it was just their usual jaunt, along with the rest of the gang. When he bought her chocolates and turned up in his best jeans and a clean

T-shirt, she'd realised something was seriously different.

Since that first awkward real date, everyone assumed they were a couple. Getting engaged last year had been what everyone expected. Both families, themselves long-standing friends, had been delighted. The fact that it had taken them so many years to decide might have been an indication of their indecision.

'Well? How did Rob take your news?' Mum insisted.

'Actually . . . '

'You haven't told him yet, have you?'

'Course not. I wanted you to be the first to know.' Sally blushed guiltily. She was no good at fibbing. She had broken the news to her mother because things were happening rather quickly.

She was putting off telling Rob as long as possible. She wanted the deal settled, so that there was no way she could be persuaded out of it. 'I'm seeing him later today. I'll tell him then.'

'He'll go bananas. You're doing the wrong thing, Sally. You can't expect him to wait for you. How long will you be gone?'

'I don't know. The contract is initially for six months, renewable if things work out. You could come over for a holiday if you want to. Dad would love it.'

Her mother frowned again.

'And just where do you think we'd get the money to afford a trip to New Zealand, for goodness sake?'

'It doesn't cost that much. I could probably help out anyway. You'd have no expenses when you were there. You could stay with me. Think of it. Trips out to see the geysers. Thermal parks. Maori culture to explore. This is truly the chance of a lifetime and you know I've always longed to travel. And they say it's such a beautiful country.'

'That's to be seen. You really should think very hard before you make your decision.'

'Actually Mum, I have made the decision. I've got visas, everything. My

4

flight's booked.'

Her mum went pale and clutched the side of her chair.

'And when exactly do you leave?' she asked in clipped tones.

'In two weeks' time. On the tenth.'

'I see. Well, I hope you'll be happy and manage to live with yourself. You are an extremely selfish girl.' Her mother's tight lips and clipped words made Sally feel as bad as she'd expected. She drew in a deep breath and spoke again.

'Mum, I am twenty-four. Most girls have left home long before my age.'

'To think, our only daughter could do this to us. I thought we'd brought you up to be more thoughtful. And Tony. He'll miss you like crazy.'

'My little brother doesn't care one jot about what I do. Since he's been away at college, I don't see him from one month's end to the next. He'll barely notice I've gone. I might even be back before he's missed me.'

'But your father and I will miss you.'

She stifled a sob. 'I can't believe it. The other side of the world. Now, I must get dinner organised.' She bustled out of the room, trying to hide her distress. The day always did have to come when her daughter left home. She'd hoped it would be to move just down the road, when she and Rob were married. There was a nice little semi for sale at the moment, just two doors down. But New Zealand. That was a very serious move. Drastic.

Sally sat staring into space. When her boss had offered her the job, she'd at first been flattered and quite against the idea. How could she possibly go off round the world and set up a new office, so far away from everything and everyone she knew?

After a couple of days, she knew it was the chance of a lifetime. She'd always dreamed of travelling. Rob often claimed that he'd like to go away too, but his idea of travel was a bus tour round Wales. Nothing at all wrong with that of course, but the world was a huge place with so much to see.

She braced herself and went to change. She was meeting Rob for a drink later on. It was not going to be a pleasant meeting.

★ ★ ★

Two weeks and three days later, she waited at Heathrow for the plane taking her on the first leg of the flight. Her first stop was Singapore, where she had a couple of hours before flying on to Auckland.

Secretly, Sally's heart was pounding. She felt a mixture of anticipation, sheer terror, excitement and all tinged with regret at leaving her family and also her now ex-fiancé. It couldn't have been worse, her meeting with Rob that fateful evening. Even now she felt close to tears at the memory.

He had exploded when she broke the news. All her statements about only being a day away, cheap phone deals and letters, none of it meant anything to him All he could see was the fact that she didn't care enough about him or their joint future to turn down a job opportunity. How could she have handled it any differently?

He'd insisted they broke off their engagement immediately and said he never wanted to see her again. She'd quietly laid the solitaire diamond ring on the table and left the pub. She walked the short distance home and went back into the accusing silence of her parents' sitting-room.

Sitting in the airport, she pulled out her mobile phone. She stared at it, wondering if it would be of any use anywhere again. She dialled home.

'All well so far,' she said to the answering machine. 'Just about to leave for the departure gate. Love you both. I'll call when I arrive in New Zealand.' Sally snapped the phone shut and dropped it into her bag. She felt very alone as she joined the queue of folks boarding the plane.

The flight to Singapore went on

forever, it seemed. She lost count of what time her body thought it was and what meal should have been next. It was bizarre to be eating breakfast and then watch a movie, only to doze off and discover it was actually dinner time. Finally, the plane touched down in the middle of a storm, amidst strings of lights that stretched away endlessly. The huge swirl of activity, the crowds, the shopping malls, the luggage trolleys, all sent her sleep deprived mind into a panic.

What was she doing? Giving up security, family, everything, to follow some stupid whim. Maybe she could get the next plane home again. She felt more alone than she ever had before. She was already missing everyone. Her parents. Rob. What had she done? Was there still time to go back?

Eventually, her mother had come to terms with the idea just a little at least. Dad had been very encouraging and urged her to make the most of this chance. He'd even agreed that he and her mother would do their best to visit.

'After all,' he'd said cheerfully, 'it isn't everyone who has the offer of free accommodation for a stay somewhere so exciting.'

'Bless you, Daddy,' she'd whispered emotionally.

There were a couple of hours to wait before her connecting flight to New Zealand. She wandered through the huge airport, marvelling at the shops. It was like a town itself with a proper shopping mall and exhibition halls. Restaurants sold exotic looking food and she began to wonder if she was missing an opportunity in not staying over for a few days. At last her onward flight was called and she boarded for her final leg.

'Thank goodness I took up this offer,' she remarked to herself. If she hadn't seized the chance, she would probably have ended up in a safe marriage, with a couple of kids in no time at all. She may never have even known what lay outside her ordered little life.

2

For much of the flight to Auckland, an exhausted Sally managed to sleep. It was shorter than the flight to Singapore and she felt less spaced out when she arrived. It was early morning as she arrived and she caught her breath flying over the huge harbour with hundreds of small boats.

'What a sight,' she said aloud to the amusement of her fellow passengers.

'Sure is. Does it for me every time,' the woman sitting next to her remarked. 'This your first trip over here?'

'Yes. You come from New Zealand?'

'Yup. Forty k. outside the city to the north.'

'Forty k?'

'Kilometres. We use metric not miles.'

'Something else for me to get used to.'

They chatted for a few moments as

the plane drew to a halt and everyone began lifting down luggage from the overhead lockers. She followed the crowd to collect her luggage and gazed round at the modern looking terminal with interest. There were displays of life in New Zealand and immediately, she felt her heart fluttering with anticipation.

Once she had cleared immigration, she had to change to another terminal for an internal flight. She had resisted the temptation to make a stopover and was going straight to Tauranga, a town on the northern coast, near to where the new office was to be sited. The Bay of Plenty, the brochures informed her. Sounded rather rural and comfortable.

Almost for the first time in days, she thought of the new office and the work that lay ahead. A whole new feeling of panic hit her. She couldn't possibly do everything her boss thought she could. How could she possibly set up a whole new office with all the complicated systems that were necessary in today's commerce? She was going to make a complete idiot of herself and she'd have to turn tail and go back home a failure.

'Come on, Sally,' she scolded herself. 'Pull yourself together. Of course you can do it. You wouldn't be here now if there was any doubt, would you? Gary would hardly trust you with his New Zealand enterprise if he thought for a moment you couldn't cope.'

By mid-morning, she had arrived in Tauranga and took a taxi for the rather longer than expected journey out to the office, where a local agent was due to meet her with the keys. The taxi left her quite some distance from the town itself, in a pleasant, fairly up-market suburb. The little office building was deserted and she stood on the pavement looking around.

After half-an-hour, she began to panic. The fitful sleep had not entirely refreshed her and suddenly, she felt desperately tired. She couldn't haul her mountain of luggage with her and nor could she leave it.

She fumbled in her bag to find details of the agent's address. It was not there. She cursed silently and delved into another of her many bags. No luck. Back to the first one and there it was after all. She was obviously getting herself into a state.

She pulled out her mobile and dialled the number. There were a few crackles and then silence. Of course. She was so used to using the phone at home, she had momentarily forgotten where she was. She glanced up and down the quiet street. There was no-one around and certainly no telephone kiosks to use. She began to feel angry. She had travelled halfway round the world and yet the wretched agent couldn't even manage to drive from the other side of town to meet her like he was supposed to. Wearily, she collected the luggage together and piled everything she could on top of the small luggage trolley that held her main suitcase.

She tottered down the road, hoping she was moving to the busier part of the area. She stood at a road junction, wondering which way to go next as a car drew up beside her. The window was lowered and a woman leaned over.

'Are you Miss Parslow, by any chance?' the woman asked.

'Yes, I am. Are you the elusive agent? I was expecting a man for some reason.'

'Leonie Barker. How do you do? I'm so sorry I was late. What a welcome for you. Do you want to put your luggage in the boot?'

'I suppose I could put the smaller bits in. I'll walk back with the other thing. It weighs a ton, but the wheels help.'

'You might as well put the lot in. I'll drive you over to the apartment when we're through here at the office.'

Gratefully, Sally loaded her things into the car boot. She'd be so pleased to unpack and find something else to wear. She felt as if she'd been living in these clothes for days. Leonie opened the office door and they went in. It was a single storey building with a largish main room and small toilet and cloakroom at the rear. It was simply furnished, with a large desk, several filing cabinets and a computer workstation to one side. Leonie busied herself opening the blinds and a window to let the air in. There was a large fan in the corner, instead of air-conditioning.

'I hope this is going to be what you need. It's small, but as you won't be carrying any actual stock here, it seemed to fulfil the spec your boss sent over.'

'It looks great to me,' Sally replied. 'Once the computer stuff is installed, we should be up and running in no time.'

'The phone is due to be connected later today and I understand you have the computer chap coming in the morning.'

'That's right. I'm not sure why Gary, my boss, thought he needed to have someone on the ground here. Most business is done over the Internet these days, but he seemed to think it was a good idea. Who am I to complain?'

'Or me. I'm running much of my own business via the Internet. I had a website made and bingo everything's been happening since. You're in the wine business aren't you?'

'That's right. I wondered whether we should have set-up in South Island as most of the wine seems to be produced there.'

'Not at all. There are plenty of vineyards in North Island. Besides, the climate's better here . . . for living that is. Much warmer.'

'I'm not complaining. It all looks good to me. And I'm grateful for the chance to see something of this side of the world.'

The two women chatted comfortably, as they left the office.

'I've got an apartment organised just a few minutes away. I assumed you wouldn't have a car so at least you can walk to the office until you decide if you need one. She stopped outside a modern, high rise building. 'It's on the third floor. At least you get a decent view of the bay from one side.'

Sally gasped, as she looked out of the living-room window. It was perfect. Her mother would be very happy once she saw a picture of this.

'It's gorgeous. Such a lovely bay. Wow. But doesn't a place like this cost an absolute fortune?'

'Your boss agreed to it. I shouldn't even bother to ask. Just enjoy it all.'

'Fine by me,' Sally said with a laugh.

'Right, I'll leave you to settle in. You have my number if you need anything. I'll help with anything I can. You can give me a call any time and don't be afraid to ask for any guidance you need. Anything at all. I hope you'll enjoy your stay.'

'Thanks very much. I'll keep in touch.'

Once she was left alone, she began to explore her new home in more detail. There was only one bedroom but the couch in the living-room opened out to make a double bed. She could manage on that, so her parents could have the bedroom, when and if they came to stay.

The kitchen was tiny but had everything she could need. Microwave, fridge freezer, washer/drier. It was beautifully organised and she felt at home immediately. There was even a jar of coffee and some milk in the fridge, thoughtfully left by Leonie. She made a cup and sat staring out at the view. She could get a surf board, she thought. Learn how to enjoy the wonderful breakers that rolled on to the beach.

She would also have to consider getting a car and very soon. There would be business trips to be made and besides, she wanted to see as much of the country as she could. At least they drove on the same side of the road here.

She jumped as the phone rang. She looked around, unsure of where the sound was coming from. It was in the kitchen.

'Hello?' she said uncertainly. Who on earth could be calling her?

'Telecom,' said the male voice. 'Your number has now been connected.'

'Oh. Right. Thanks very much.'

'The number's unchanged from the previous tenants. Should be written on the equipment somewhere. You'll find the contract in the apartment. Sign and return it as soon as you can. Thanks ma'am.'

She saw a bundle of papers and found the right sheet. She realised she could now call home and tell her parents she had arrived safely and had settled. A glance at her watch and a few calculations told her it was well past midnight at home. A call now would not be popular with her parents. A small pang of homesickness hit her as she thought of her parents in their own comfortable home. This was a lovely place, but it was not yet home. She chided herself.

'This is your big adventure, Sally Parslow. Don't start getting maudlin.'

She hauled herself to her feet, took her case into the bedroom and began to unpack. Everything was showing the signs of having been crammed into a suitcase for several days. She found some towels and went into the bathroom to shower. It felt wonderful, as the warm powerful jet sprayed over her tired body. She realised she was very hungry and there was nothing to eat in the apartment. Before she fell asleep where she stood, she needed to find a shop and stock up.

Unable to resist the temptation, she crossed over the busy road to the beach. The smell of the sea was exciting. She had never lived close to any sort of water and this was quite magical. She had to be firm with herself and go and find shops. Reluctantly, she turned away and made for what looked like a fairly busy street.

Most shops were rather touristy and beach oriented. There were several cafes and ice cream parlours. Maybe something to eat there was a better idea than cooking at home. She realised with a thrill that she had actually called it home. After she had eaten, she discovered that there was a small convenience store along the next road.

A light was flashing on the phone when she returned home. She picked it up and a voice told her she had one message waiting. A pleasant male voice sounded in her ear.

'Hi, Miss Parslow. Adam Edwards here. Computer Services. I am due to visit your office tomorrow morning but I'm afraid I have a problem. Would you call me back please and we'll arrange a time to meet up.' He then left a number and she grabbed a pen to make a note.

She punched in the numbers. She was ready to insist on prompt service. The computer was essential and she must have it immediately. Maybe they weren't used to getting things done quickly here. It wouldn't do.

'Adam Edwards,' the voice said on the other end.

'Mr Edwards. It's Sally Parslow, returning your call.'

'Look, I'm really sorry. It's very

unprofessional of me. A family problem. There's nothing I can do.'

'But I can do nothing until the machine's up and running. It's extremely urgent. I have to get back in contact with my head office as fast as possible. Let's face it, you only got the job because you could promise personal, fast service. It's a highly competitive world you know.'

'Tell me about it. Look, as I said, I'm really sorry. My little boy has to go to the hospital and I can't avoid it. I should be back later on in the morning, but you can never tell exactly how these appointments will go. Sorry. I'm not playing the sympathy card. I'm stuck with a situation.'

'I do sympathise, but it doesn't help my situation.' She sounded so horrid. So professional. So . . . nothing matters but me.

'I'll tell you what. Are you busy this evening? I could get a sitter once Brad's in bed. Then I could come over to see what the layout is, this evening. Could even get started.'

'OK. You're on,' Sally agreed. She forgot she was feeling as if she could drop with exhaustion and perked up immediately.

She replaced the receiver and went to collect keys. She wondered briefly why his wife couldn't attend the hospital with the child. At least, she consoled herself, Gary would have been proud of her. Maybe he'd suspected she had a ruthless side to her character, when he appointed her as his New Zealand representative. She had learned a lot about the wine business through the five years she'd worked with Gary. She'd taken a course in business management but had rapidly become interested in the product itself, rather than just managing accounts and all the rest. She'd taken a course in wine appreciation, much to her father's amusement.

Dear Dad, she thought suddenly and once more felt pangs of homesickness. It was still too early to phone them and let them know she'd arrived safely. She wondered how Rob was getting on. She felt strange knowing that she had left him so far away. It was the first time in ten, no, eleven years that she hadn't been going out with Rob.

Sally walked the short distance to the office and let herself in. It was dark and she fumbled to find the light switch. The place looked very empty. No clutter or personal bits and pieces to make it look homely. There was a huge peg board area on the wall. She could put up some posters of the wine growing regions to make it look more cheerful.

There was a knock on the door. She crossed to open it. The computer man. Adam something . . . Edwards, that was it.

'Come in, Mr Edwards. Sally Parslow,' she announced as she held out her hand.

'Hi. Adam. Call me Adam. Sorry to give so much hassle. I'm not normally quite so unprofessional.'

Sally studied him. Around thirty. Quite tall. Mid brown hair, with blond bits where the sun had caught it. His light blue eyes were very striking in the tanned face. His handshake was firm and his smile most attractive. She knew immediately that they would get on well.

'I'm sorry,' Sally apologised, realising she had been so busy summing him up, she hadn't spoken for several seconds. 'This is the office,' she added unnecessarily.

'I guessed it might be,' he replied with a huge grin. 'Now, where do you want your work area to be?'

'Where it is I suppose. There's not much choice is there?'

'You could swing the room round the other way. Have the main desk facing the door and your computer against the wall. That way, you can see anyone approaching before they open the door.'

'That's a good idea. Oh dear. I'm not much use, am I? I hadn't given a thought to any of this.'

'You've only just flown in, haven't you? Give yourself a chance.' He smiled again and she felt her heart give a lurch. He was quite disarming. His accent was also appealing. All the vowel sounds seemed changed around, similar, but not quite the same as the Australian twang she was familiar with from the soaps she watched at home.

She forced herself to take a deep breath. He was possibly the first new male she had encountered since Rob. But, he had a child and that placed him well-beyond anything more than an office contact. Good grief, whatever had come over her? She was behaving like some total idiot. It must be the jet-lag.

'I'm sorry, but I haven't got anything organised. I can't even offer you a coffee. No kettle. No cups. Nothing.'

'Good job I'm only here to do a recce then, isn't it? I don't function without a caffeine fix every now and then.'

'I'll go shopping tomorrow. By the time you get back here, we'll be up and running. Coffee on tap.'

'Good. Now, your boss specified

most of the equipment he wanted installed. It's just a case of getting it brought over. I've assembled most of the computer, but needed to check on various pieces of software you'll need.'

'You've built it? What, actually put it together?'

'Course. That's how most computers are made. The customer explains what they want to do with it and the dealer goes away and makes it. It won't take much installing. The main lines are here already.' He picked up the phone. 'When do you get connected?'

'Tomorrow I expect. The agent was organising that.'

'Great. Look, I don't know what time I'll be through at the hospital tomorrow, but if you really don't mind giving up another evening, I can definitely be here after normal working hours.'

'Fine. The sooner the better. I hope it's nothing too serious wrong with your son?'

'He has asthma. It's just a general medical. We're part of a research project, so it's important to turn up whenever we're summoned. I usually work from home so there isn't much of a problem. Just unfortunate that you and his appointment clashed this time.'

Sally was burning to ask about his wife, but felt it might seem too nosy. She bit back her questions. He smiled at her again and she found herself blushing once more.

'Can I take you for a coffee?' he offered.

'Don't you have to get home?'

'I have a sitter till ten. After that, I turn into a pumpkin. That gives us a clear hour.'

'OK. That would be very nice.' Sally knew she couldn't refuse, but waves of tiredness were washing over her.

She got into his car and fastened the safety belt. It was rather an elderly vehicle and she noticed the back was littered with toys and a few empty crisp packets and an old drink can. He was obviously a family man.

'Sorry about the mess. I always keep

meaning to clear it out, but somehow it never seems the most important priority.'

'Know what you mean. Is your wife away?' She never meant to say anything, but her thoughts were ranging round his comment about babysitters and working from home.

'She works in Auckland.'

'I see. That must be very hard for you both.'

'I manage. Now, have you found Georgio's yet? Best coffee anywhere.'

'I haven't found anything yet. Least of all shops. Where do I go to stock up?'

'I'll show you on the way home. It isn't far. Bayfair shopping mall's the nearest. Everything you need's there. Where are you staying, by the way?'

'Just along this road. Walking distance of the office. I don't have a car yet, so major shopping will be difficult for a while.' They chatted easily about the town and various entertainments to look out for. She really liked him and found herself comparing him to Rob more than a few times.

'Must be difficult for your son, only seeing his mother at weekends.'

'Brad copes very well,' was all he would say on the subject.

'How old is he?'

'Six. But he's a bit behind at school with the asthma and all. He doesn't take too much time off. They don't encourage it nowadays. He has his puffers of course and usually manages to control it.'

'Your car will be turning into its pumpkin form, if we don't make a move,' Sally said, glancing at her watch.

'Heavens. Hadn't realised the time had passed so quickly. I've enjoyed meeting you, Sally. Thanks for a pleasant evening.'

'Thank you for the coffee. You're right. It's certainly very good coffee. I'll never match up to this in the office.'

'I haven't got round to showing you the shopping centre. Tomorrow night, maybe?'

'See how it goes. I can always get a

cab or something. I realise I shall have to get a car as soon as possible. Maybe I should look at something tomorrow.'

'Leave it till the weekend and I'll take you over to a friend of mine. He's got a car dealership. He'll be able to sort you out.'

'But your wife. The weekend is when she comes home, surely?'

'Not this weekend. We'll discuss the car tomorrow. I'd better go now. See you then.' He drove away quickly, leaving her standing on the pavement, staring after him.

'If only . . . ' she whispered regretfully. 'I could really like him.'

3

Sally could never remember feeling so weary. She just about managed to dial her parents to let them know her new number and that she had arrived safely before she collapsed in a heap.

'I'll call tomorrow, Mum,' she said. 'I'm practically falling asleep where I stand.'

'But I want to hear all about your flat and your journey, of course.'

'Tomorrow, Mum. Promise. Its half-past ten here and I haven't slept properly for days.'

'You don't sound far away at all,' Mum went on, obviously relishing the idea of talking to her daughter right at the other side of the world.

In desperation, Sally practically put the phone down while she was speaking. She fell into bed and knew nothing more till eleven o'clock the next morning. She awoke with a start, when she realised the sun was streaming into her room. She sat up and looked at her watch.

'Good grief. How can I have slept so long?' It was a good job Adam was busy this morning. She added an alarm clock to her growing list of essential shopping.

It was almost five before she finally unlocked the door to the office. She had taken a bus to the shopping mall and bought so much that she needed a cab to return home. It seemed strange to see familiar products in the shops and she had several moments wondering why things suddenly cost so much more, until she remembered she was dealing in New Zealand dollars.

Some prices actually seemed very low and she stocked up on rather more than she might have done. She had brought a few essentials for the office and had loaded everything into her suitcase to wheel it on her luggage trolley. As

Adam arrived, he looked at the case and smiled.

'Leaving already?' he asked. 'Couldn't stand the pace, I guess.' His accent was not strong, but noticeable and very attractive, Sally thought.

'I did so much shopping, it was the easiest way to get it here. How was the hospital?'

'Good. It all went very well. We're now cleared for the next six months, barring accidents.'

'Must be a relief to you.'

'Certainly is. Brad's back at school tomorrow so I won't be under quite such pressure. Well, I'd better make a start. Is the phone connected yet?'

Sally went to pick it up and heard the welcome dialling tone.

'Great.' Adam said. 'We can get the links sorted and you can be in touch with your boss in no time.'

'No more excuses for slacking then. I can ask him about a car and get myself really organised.'

'I spoke to my pal. He's got several in

at the moment. Are you free Saturday morning? I can drive you over there and you can have the dubious pleasure of meeting my little son, Brad. You're not allergic to kids, are you?'

She laughed. 'Not that I know of. I usually managed to survive visits from various cousins back home.'

'Excellent. He's quite user-friendly actually. Seems to have inherited his mother's charm and none of my bad habits.'

'I'll look forward to meeting him. What does your wife do?'

'Do?' he repeated.

'Work. You said she worked away. In Auckland.'

'Oh. She's a lecturer. Biology. Bright lady.' He sounded distracted and almost as if he didn't want to talk about her. Perhaps he was just missing her, Sally decided. She wouldn't rub salt into the wound by persisting in finding out more. Let him tell me if and when he feels like it.

Adam began to bring in various

boxes. She busied herself arranging some of the items she'd bought earlier. She'd bought a couple of mugs, plates and basic cutlery in addition to the essential kettle. Coffee, dried milk and sugar and some biscuits and she was all set. The cloakroom area had a small sink with a draining board. She could easily bring herself snack lunches.

'Won't you get lonely working here all alone?' Adam called to her.

'Shouldn't think so. Be nice to get on without interruptions all the time. Besides, I shall have to do a certain amount of travelling round. I hope to visit South Island before too long. Make personal contact with our suppliers.'

'I suppose you're very knowledgeable about wines.'

'I know something. Not a true connoisseur by any means. I'm not one of these types who can sniff at the cork and tell you which bush the grapes grew on.'

'Thank heavens for that. I'd never

dare ask you out otherwise.'

Sally went back into the main room. She stared at Adam. Whatever could he mean, about asking her out?

'What did you mean?'

'About what?'

'About asking me out.' She felt her colour rising again.

'Nothing. Just thought you might like to eat out sometime.'

'Adam, I don't know what impression you have formed of me, but I'm not the sort of woman who goes out with married men. I'll be grateful for your help in finding a car, but please, spare me the embarrassment . . .'

'You've got it wrong. About me and Maria. I was only being friendly. Not suggesting anything sinister.'

'Forget it now. Please. I'll let you get on with your work. I have some stuff to sort out.' She tried to look busy with various bundles of paper she had brought in with her. They were unimportant, but she could spend time filing them, anything to look active and efficient.

Adam continued to unpack the boxes. At any other time, she would have joined in with enthusiasm, opening packages as if they were presents. She saw a scanner, printer and various other parts being placed on the desk. She watched as he took out the computer itself, carefully attaching the many leads. Finally, her curiosity overcame her need to stay away from him.

'Is that a camera?' she asked, seeing the box still on the desk.

'Yes. A digital one. Gary thought it may be useful to send various pictures to him. You can use it with the computer and e-mail straight away.'

'Wow. That will be so great.' She was not thinking of Gary or work, so much as her parents. She could print out pictures of everything including ones of herself. Her parents would be delighted and maybe, they'd stop missing her so much.

'I can show you how to use it, once the programme's installed.'

'Whatever did we do without computers?' she murmured. 'Really makes
the world shrink.'

He worked steadily and was soon
ready to switch on and begin to set
things up on the machine.

'Think I'll have to call it a night. I'm
bushed. You got time for a coffee?'

'I can make you some if you like.
Only powdered milk though. Haven't
got anywhere to keep fresh.'

'I can get you a little fridge if you
want it. My parents have a camping
store. They supply them.'

'Is there anything you can't get?'
Sally laughed. 'Do you know someone
for everything anyone can possibly
need?'

'Guess so. I can find a supplier for
most things. It's a pretty small town, all
said and done.'

'I suppose everyone knows everyone
else in a place this size. Surely, that
must make you extra careful about
gossip as well? Anyhow, thanks for the
offer. I'll see.'

'We could go to Georgio's again.' She stared at him blankly for a moment. 'Coffee? Or you can make some. You choose.'

'Same place two nights on the run? It could ruin your reputation forever.'

'My reputation's shot to pieces anyhow. So, it doesn't matter.'

'I'll put the kettle on,' she said firmly. 'I need to check that it works.' She didn't know whether to believe him or not. She recognised the fact that she was attracted to him and also recognised that it was totally wrong.

'Do you surf?' Adam asked from behind her. She was spooning coffee into the cups and gave a start.

'On the water or the Internet?' He gave her a look. She grinned back. 'I've never tried. Water, that is. But I did think it looked like fun and even good exercise, maybe. I'll probably give it a try while I'm here. Get myself a board.'

'My parents . . . '

'I know. They can sell me one at a special price.' They both laughed.

'Depends on how long I'm here.'

'Sounds as if you don't intend staying.'

'I've agreed to stay for six months, initially. It may become permanent, but it depends on how things go. My parents might never forgive me.'

'You're an only child?'

'I have a brother, but he's usually away and always involved in everything that's going around him with little or no time to spare.'

'And is there someone special for you to go back?'

'There was, but that's all over. Mum's terrified I'll fall for some sheep farmer and disappear into the wilderness forever.'

'There are more things in New Zealand than sheep and sheep farmers, despite the reputation. S'pose it's inevitable that anyone from overseas believes there're nothing but sheep.'

'I haven't seen a single sheep since I arrived, come to think of it.' She laughed.

'I should go. I'll see you in the morning. We'll soon get everything sorted and the fax machine set up. A few more bits to show you and that's it. We're all done.'

He left her in the office. She wandered round, touched everything as if she could sense the essence of the man from the machines. Maybe it was simply that he'd been kind to her when she was a stranger in town. But she sensed that in different circumstances, Adam Edwards was someone she could have grown very fond of.

With a small sigh, she locked up and went home. She phoned her parents again and spoke briefly to Gary in the office. He was delighted with the progress and when she broached the idea of getting a car, he immediately agreed. He suggested she might try leasing one, instead of buying outright, just in case things didn't work out. She had to admit that she was looking forward to seeing Adam the next day.

'Come on. I'll buy you lunch,' he

offered at the end of the morning when his work was finished. Sally hesitated.

'I ought to start work properly,' she told him.

'Even the most dedicated employees are entitled to a lunch break. I know a nice little Italian place, just a few kilometres away.'

'OK,' she agreed, suspecting she was probably playing with fire. It was purely a business arrangement, she convinced herself.

They drove for about ten kilometres. Adam pulled up outside what looked like a glorified, large wooden shed.

'It may not look like much from the outside but believe me, the pasta is to die for.'

They went inside. It was cheerful with inevitable red checked table cloths and candles in bottles. There was one large room, divided into booths so diners could have the sense of privacy. A large jolly looking woman came from the back, wiping her hands on her apron.

'G'day, Adam. Don't usually see you at this time of day.'

'Hi, Anna. I needed to impress my client here. Sally Parslow, meet Anna.'

The woman had dark hair, fastened back with a ribbon. She had laughing brown eyes and held out her hand to Sally.

'Hi, Sally. Good to meet you.'

'Hello, Anna. Pleased to meet you.'

'You're from overseas? Lovely accent. Welcome to New Zealand. This your first trip?'

They chatted happily for several minutes before Anna gave them both a menu. She brought a jug of water, a dish of olives and a plate of thin bread sticks. Sally struggled to remember words of Italian from a family holiday, years ago. Finally, she had to concede defeat.

'I can't work out anything. You'd better order for me. You know what's good to eat here, I'm sure.'

'OK,' Adam agreed. 'Anything you don't like?'

She shook her head. He ordered several dishes, far too much for a lunchtime snack, Sally thought. He also ordered a carafe of wine. So much for work this afternoon, she thought, but who's to care? Gary wouldn't be in the office at this time of day, so she could always work later in the evening. She settled down to enjoy the meal and the company. After Adam had driven her back to the office, they sat outside for several minutes. It seemed as if he didn't want to leave.

'What time can you be ready on Saturday?' he asked.

'Oh, I forgot all about it. Gary suggested I lease a car rather than buy one. In case things don't work out.'

'Makes sense. S'pose my friend might still be able to help. I'll give him a call. I'll pick you up at your place around ten. How does that sound?'

'Well, if you're sure. Thanks. I'll look forward to it. And many thanks for all your work and for the delicious lunch.'

'Entirely my pleasure,' he said softly.

For a moment, Sally thought he was moving to kiss her. She blushed as her heart pounded. She very much wanted him to kiss her, but she simply could not let it happen. She collected her bag and struggled to open the car door. He leaned across her and released the catch. The thought of Rob flashed into her mind. Never had she felt this sort of chemistry between them. But it was too late for Adam.

'Thanks again,' she called out, turning to let herself into the office and get away from a situation that was already becoming too difficult to handle. She raised a cursory hand as he drove away. She found she was trembling when she closed the door behind her. She couldn't spend time alone with this man again. She'd have to find an excuse to cancel Saturday's excursion.

When Saturday arrived, she hadn't thought of any sound reason to cancel the trip. When Adam was late arriving, she began to think he had changed his mind. She dialled his number, intent on telling him not to bother.

'Thank heavens you called. I've been ringing the office number ever since last night. I must have mislaid your home number. You never told me where you live.'

'How stupid of me. I'm so sorry. Look, Adam, I've . . . '

'It doesn't matter. Brad's nearly bursting himself with curiosity. He thinks that someone from the UK is an alien of some sort!'

She gave her address to him and despite herself, knew that she was looking forward to the trip to find her a car. When she saw Brad, she fell instantly in love with him. He was so like his father, it was like seeing Adam as a child. They had the same coloured eyes and hair and exactly the same expressions on their faces as he solemnly shook hands with the alien from the UK.

'She looks quite ordinary, just the same as everyone else, doesn't she,

Dad?' he whispered slightly too loudly. Sally laughed.

'You haven't seen me when my nose goes blue or the ten arms and legs I have hidden under my jacket.' For a brief moment he looked startled and then he laughed.

'You aren't ordinary at all. You're very nice and I want you to be my friend forever. Will you, Sally? I can call you Sally, can't I?'

'I don't know what else you'd call me.' She laughed.

'And will you be my friend? As well as Daddy's friend?'

'Of course,' she said, a warm glow covering her entire body at the child's words. She smiled shyly at Adam as she got into the car.

Adam's friend, Mike, was most helpful. He was part of a group who leased cars for various periods of time, long or short term. He could get hold of exactly the sort of vehicle she wanted and agreed to arrange the whole thing by early the following week. The deal was finished soon after eleven and the rest of the day was free.

'I don't think you've actually seen anything of the locality yet, have you?' Adam asked.

'Not really. Apart from my exciting bus trip to the shopping mall, I've really done nothing.'

'Let's go to stinky city, Dad. Sally will love the pong. It's gross.'

'Rotorua it is then, unless you've any other ideas?' Adam asked.

'Maybe you've got something you need to do. I don't expect you to give up your Saturday just for me.'

'We want to go out, don't we, Dad? We always go out somewhere on the weekend,' Brad chimed in.

'Course. Unless you wanted to do something else.'

Sally shook her head. Until she had her own transport, she was up to date with work, so far.

'So why stinky city?'

'It's usually called Sulphur City, for obvious reasons. It's only about forty minutes away. OK everyone? Seat belts fastened?'

They drove along wide roads towards the South and soon, were out of sight of building and driving through forests of pine trees. Mountains loomed in the distance through clearings in the trees and there were streams and lakes to break up the miles of trees. Sally was totally enraptured by such beautiful scenery. As they approached Rotorua, the roads became busier and more tourist attractions appeared. White water rafting seemed favourite.

'Wow, I've never done that, have you?' she asked.

'Only once. Quite terrifying. Thrilling too. But I'm a family man. Can't take such risks, can I, Brad?'

'No way. Dad's had to grow up, see,' he added conversationally to Sally. She grinned as Adam gave a wink. 'He used to be a bit silly, but he has responsibilities now. Me, that is.'

She smiled at his words. Brad seemed so much older than his six years.

They drove into the town and parked at the side of a road near to the lake. The grass around the lakes was covered in a mass of black swans and other waterfowl.

'Have we got any bread, Dad?' Brad inquired.

'No, but it isn't very good for them. Everyone feeds them bread. How many ducks or geese do you know who go to the baker's regularly?'

Brad roared with laughter. It was infectious and soon the trio were smiling happily as they wandered towards the water.

'It's a lovely lake, isn't it? I don't know why you thought it smelled so bad. It's fine here.'

'Depends which way the wind blows,' Adam told her. 'We'll take you to look at some of the thermal areas later. Now, can you see over there? There's a large mountain right back there. That's Mount Tarawera. It's a volcano. Blew just over a hundred years ago. Buried a village. That's another must see place.

Fascinating, as well as horrific to think of. New Zealand's answer to Pompeii.'

'Heavens. There's so much to take in. What are the planes for?' she asked, pointing at a row of white aircraft with water skis attached instead of undercarriages.

'They do flights over the volcano and around. Something else you might think about some day. Pretty pricey, but an amazing trip. Now, who's for something to eat? I'm starving. There's a café over there. Shall we see what they've got?'

Brad slipped his hand into Sally's and the other into his father's. Looking like any other family, they swung him along as they crossed to the café.

'I'm glad you came to New Zealand, Sally,' Brad announced.

'I reckon I'm glad too,' she murmured in reply.

4

'You must let me pay for the food this time,' Sally insisted. 'You can't keep treating me and taking me out everywhere.'

'But we always go out somewhere on Saturdays, don't we, Dad?' Adam nodded.

'I thought you might see your mummy on Saturdays.' The words slipped out before she realised what she was saying.

'Mummy's usually too busy to see me,' Brad said. 'But I don't mind. Me and Dad have much more fun.'

'I see,' Sally muttered. 'So you live here most of the time, then?'

'Maria has a busy social life as well as work. Does a lot of fundraisers and other public events. It works out best for Brad this way.'

The subject clearly was one which he

didn't want to speak about and for Brad's sake, she too let the subject drop. All the same it was most intriguing and she wanted to know more. When they'd finished toasted sandwiches and eaten a large ice-cream each, they left the small restaurant and walked further round the pretty lake. The smell of sulphur was beginning to be more noticeable as the wind was stirring.

'I see what you mean about the smell. What is it exactly?'

'The whole area's sitting on an area of thermal activity. Tell you what. Shall we go and take a look at one of the parks? There's a big one just a short distance at the side of the town. Goes by the delightful name of Whakarewarewa.'

'Good grief. I'll never get my mouth round these Maori names. OK. If you're sure. Whak-a-what-ever you said, it is.'

It was a fascinating afternoon and Sally was totally captured by the extraordinary sight of steam pouring out of holes in the ground and pools of near boiling water. The smell of sulphur was all around, but it became less oppressive as they got used to it.

'I'm not sure I shall ever get used to seeing steam pouring out of a bunker on the golf course,' she laughed. 'Aren't you always afraid it's going to explode into a huge volcanic eruption?'

'You get used to it. There are places where one needs to be cautious and the character of the ground does change, but there are warnings given if anything big could happen. The last one was Ruapehu, further south, in about 1995. That one destroyed the skiing for a few years. And there's White Island out in the bay that has a flurry from time to time.'

Sally stared around and decided it must be country that was still evolving. The largely uncontrollable heat beneath the ground had given rise to a landscape that was quite alien to her, after living her life in rural England. Dramatically beautiful, she had already fallen in love with her new home.

'Thank you so much for introducing me to all this. I can't wait to explore the whole area. I must let you get home now. I've taken up enough of your time.'

Brad was tugging at his father's arm and desperately trying to whisper something. Adam laughed and chided him for whispering in public.

'But, Daddy,' he persisted. 'I want to ask you something.'

'Go on.' He nodded apologetically to Sally and bent down to put his ear next to Brad's mouth. 'Well, I don't know. She may not want to. You'd better ask, hadn't you?'

'Please, Sally, will you come and have supper with us? Please.'

'Well . . . I shouldn't inflict myself on you for much longer. You've given up your entire day for me. I feel guilty.'

'No. We always go out on Saturdays. I told you. And it was much better having you here too. Cos even though we've seen everything already it seems new when you see it. Please come.'

She looked at Adam who was grinning. He nodded his agreement.

'I can't promise a gourmet supper, but you're welcome to share our frozen chicken special.'

Her every instinct told her to refuse the invitation, but what did she have to go home for? Something on television and a snack from her own freezer. It was no contest and she accepted gratefully, even though it meant Adam would either have to take her home and organise a sitter or she would have to get a taxi. She had to admit, she was intrigued to see for herself the family set up and the home where this lovely man and his adorable son were living.

It was a pleasant evening. Brad asked Sally to read his bedtime story and laughed at her English accent, especially when she faltered over some of the New Zealand place names.

'Will you tell me about England next time?' he begged. 'Tell me some English stories?'

'I expect you know a lot of them already,' she murmured, wondering what on earth a six-year-old would be reading from her own limited knowledge of children. Besides, she didn't want to become too involved with Brad, especially as her own time and stay in New Zealand was limited. 'I must go now and you need to go to sleep.'

'Can we all go out again next weekend? It was the best, having you with us today.'

'Night,' she said kissing his soft forehead and stroking the soft brown curls with blond tips, just like his father's.

There was a photograph of a dark haired woman on his chest of drawers. She was very beautiful but had a smile that looked somehow, artificial.

'Is that your mummy?' she asked without thinking.

'Daddy says I should keep her picture there so I remember what she looks like.'

'She's very beautiful,' Sally said with

a slight grudging note in her voice.

'You're prettier,' Brad said with a grin.

'Night, night,' she murmured and kissed the top of his head. She felt warmed by his words, even if they weren't true.

'I'd better be off myself,' she said once she had re-joined Adam in the lounge room. 'Can I order a taxi?'

'I'll see if Betty from next door can pop round for ten minutes. I can easily drive you.'

'Nonsense. I won't hear of you getting a sitter for that.'

'She won't mind. Adores Brad and lives alone so she's glad of a change of scene. We could have a drink. Or some coffee? Unless you really have had enough of us for one day.'

'Oh, Adam, don't be silly. You've been wonderful and I've loved my day with you. But we can't go on like this. You have a wife. I'm only here for a relatively short time. It isn't fair to any of us. Especially to Brad. He's gorgeous and I don't want to let him get any closer and then leave him when I go back to England. It wouldn't be fair.'

He gave a shrug and didn't argue any more. He looked up a local taxi company in the phone book and dialled the number.

As she left the house, she looked back and waved. Maybe she felt a tad disappointed that he hadn't argued a little more strongly. But that was right. He had to realise there was no future for them, whatever the state of his marriage. Reading between the lines, he and . . . what was her name? Maria? . . . certainly had some sort of problem. What mother could be too busy to see her own child, even at weekends?

It was nine o'clock when she arrived back at her flat. She made a calculation and decided it would be eight o'clock in the morning at home. It was a good time to call her parents.

'Hello, Mum. Only me.'

'Oh, Sally, Darling.' She turned to call her husband in great excitement.

'It's Sally. Oh, Jack, it's Sally. All the way from New Zealand.'

'So I should hope,' she heard her father's voice mutter.

'How are you? Is everything going well? What's the weather like? Have you got a nice apartment? Have you been out anywhere nice? What are the people like? Friendly? How's the job?'

'Oh, Mum. You never change. Let me get a word in and I'll tell you everything.' It was easy to tell her parents about her flat, her job and about visiting Rotorua. The fact that she'd been there with Adam and Brad was left hazy.

'Oh what an experience for you, Darling. Make the most of it all, won't you?' her mother suggested.

'I intend to. It's such a wonderful country. You must think about coming over before I leave. If I do leave. And no, I haven't met any sheep farmers so you've no worries there.'

'This call must be costing you a fortune. But it's so lovely to chat. It doesn't seem possible that you are right round the other side of the world.'

'Like I said, Mum. We're really only a day away.'

'I suppose so. Take care love. I'd better start on breakfast.'

'I'm just about to go to bed. Weird isn't it? Love you both,' she said as she put the phone down. However much the call cost, it was well worth it to keep in touch and she knew it would mean a lot to her parents. She must take some pictures and send them very soon.

She lay in bed, reflecting on the day. It had been good to spend time with Adam and Brad, but she mustn't let it become a habit. They seemed to have enjoyed her company, but she couldn't forget that he was married and she wasn't allowed to become fond of either Brad or his father. It was very strange though. Neither of them seemed to want to speak about Maria or their relationship and the woman clearly had scant contact with her son.

Once the office was running as she

wanted, Sally decided it was time to begin her travels around looking at the various wine suppliers in the immediate area. Her little car was running perfectly after Mike had delivered it to her flat in person, a few days ago. It seemed everything was going pretty much as she'd hoped.

She began by visiting retail outlets and familiarising herself with the most popular wines on the shelves. She did get a few odd looks when she took out a notebook to write down various names and vineyards she intended to check out. She hoped to pick out some of the smaller places whose names were less familiar in Britain and hopefully, to be able to raise their profile while the prices were still low.

She visited several small towns nearby and returned to the office late in the afternoon to type up the information she had collected. She switched on the computer and waited. It bleeped and whirred a couple of times and then stopped working altogether. She tried again. This time nothing worked at all.

She pulled the plug out and plugged it in again, desperate to try anything. There was only one thing for it. She must phone Adam and get him to come and sort it out. After all her firm resolutions, she needed to contact him again. He was delighted to receive her call.

'I thought we'd put you off completely,' he began. 'So, have you relented and are allowing us to see you again soon?'

'Well, er . . . actually, the computer's died on me.'

'Died in what way?'

'As in not working. Nothing. Can you come round?' There was a pause. He covered the phone and she could hear a muttering in the background.

'Hi? I've got a bit of a problem. It's Brad. He's off school again. Got a slight cold and with his asthma, I have to be careful or it easily turns to something much worse.'

'I see. So what do you suggest?'

'I could bring him along with me. He's not too bad actually and certainly not infectious or anything.'

Sally took a deep breath while she thought. She really needed her computer to be working. In fact, if it had been anyone but Adam who'd provided it, she would have been angry that it had failed so soon.

'Well,' she said doubtfully, 'I suppose it'd be all right. If you're sure it won't make him any worse.'

'Oh no. He'll be all right. He'd love to come and see you again. Seems you made something of a hit. He's not usually too good with women so it's quite a compliment to you.' Before she knew it, they were on their way over. Brad ran into the office and gave her a hug. Adam followed, looking slightly sheepish. He smiled hesitantly.

'So what's going on with this machine? Can't believe it's gone crook on ya.'

'Gone crook?'

'Not working. Let's have a look.' He

pulled the machine out and peered into the back. He fiddled with the cables and sockets and tried switching it on. Everything seemed quite dead. 'Strange,' he muttered. He produced a test meter and tried the socket. 'That's dead too. Think you've got a fuse somewhere. Is there anything new in the electric line you've plugged in?'

'Only the kettle, but I've been using it all week.'

He tried each socket in turn and finally went to the fuse box. After testing the various fuses, he nodded and repaired it. He then moved to the various appliances and tested them.

'Afraid it's this kettle that's the culprit. Faulty connection on it. Must have blown the fuse and then set off everything else. I just hope it hasn't damaged the computer. You say you got some sort of noise when you switched on?'

'It sort of bleeped and whirred and then went phut.'

Brad giggled. He was still standing

with his arms round her waist, hugging her as if he couldn't let go.

'Phut, phut, phut,' he called and began to rush round the office as he chanted the words.

'Cool it, Brad, boy. You'll only get wheezy again.'

'I'm all right now. Phut, phut,' he added for good measure.

'OK. So here's what I think happened. You got a faulty kettle and must have been lucky the first few times you used it. It finally gave up and fused the whole circuit.

'Let's hope we've been lucky with the computer and the whole thing isn't a write off.'

Sally went white.

'The whole thing?' she echoed.

'Sensitive creatures, computers. We may be lucky. The power must have surged briefly before the fuse finally went. Let's give it a go.'

He plugged the machine in and waited for a moment. There were several clicks and whirs and the computer sprang into life. It had to perform several processes before it was ready to use again and Adam smiled in satisfaction.

'There you go. All up and running with no major problems. But I should take that kettle back to wherever you bought it. It's downright dangerous. You want me to go with you?'

'Course not. I'm more than capable of telling them what I think of their lousy product. Sorry, but I can't even offer you a cup of coffee now.'

'Look, I think you should put in a safety device. Something to protect the computer if there's a power cut or a fuse goes. It will enable you to switch the machine off without any problems.'

'OK. But have you got one of these things, whatever it is.'

'It's called a UPS. Sure. But I'll have to go to the store and buy it. I would go now, but I don't really want to drag Brad with me.'

'He can stay here with me if you like. If you trust me to look after him. I should warn you though, I'm not at all used to children, especially ones with asthma.'

'I'd only take half-an-hour or so. If you're both happy with that, I'm OK with it too. What do you say, Braddy boy?' The little boy nodded happily.

'OK then. I'll go to the store and see what I can find. Be good, won't you?' He strode out of the small office and got into his car and sped off down the road.

'So, what shall we do?' Sally was hesitant. What did six-year-old boys like to do? Now she was on her own with him, she felt slightly nervous.

'Tell me about where you live. In England, I mean.'

For fifteen minutes or so, she entertained him with stories of the little Midlands town where she'd live all her life. She told him about the puppy she'd had for her seventh birthday and the fun they'd had in the local park. Maybe she exaggerated things a little to make them funnier, but she realised how much she appreciated having a good childhood and caring parents.

'I wish I could have a puppy,' Brad said wistfully. 'But Daddy says I can't cos of my asthma.'

'Yes, I guess it wouldn't be a good idea if it made you feel ill all the time. But maybe you'll grow out of it one day.'

'My mummy says I won't. She should know cos she's a sort of doctor.'

'I thought she was a sort of teacher.'

'She's a lecturer at the hospital. She does work as a sort of doctor too, sometimes.'

'I see. How much do you see your mummy?' she asked, trying to sound casual.

'Not much. She's always very busy,' he added defensively.

'What, once a fortnight? Once a month?'

'I don't know. When she isn't too busy. I think I saw her near Christmas.'

'But that's simply ages ago. Haven't you seen her since then?' She blurted the words out before she could stop herself, so shocked was she. He shook his head but showed no signs of being upset.

Sally tried to think of something else to talk about, but her mind was filled with thoughts about the state of Adam's marriage. They played a couple of games of noughts and crosses and just as they finished, Adam came back. She gave a quiet sigh of relief.

'Sorry. Took longer than I'd expected. Hope he hasn't been a problem?'

'Course not. We've had a good chat, haven't we?'

'Did you know, Sally had her very own puppy when she was little?'

'Really,' Adam said. 'That's nice. Now, we need to plug this little device into the back of your machine and route some cables round the back.' Soon he was absorbed in his task and with an occasional grunt and mumbled words that nobody could hear or understand, he finally stood up. 'Reckon that should make you fool proof. It bleeps if the power goes off and that gives you time to shut everything down.'

'Great. Thank you very much. You'll have to send the bill and I'll get a cheque made out.'

Brad had been very quiet during this episode and finally he ran to his father and whispered something.

'Please,' he said out loud. 'Ask her now.' Adam shrugged.

'OK, but don't blame me if she says no. Seems my son would like a date with you.'

'I see,' Sally laughed. 'And where would he like to go on this date?'

'Out on Saturday. Out to the mountains.'

'It really depends on how you are. We won't be going anywhere if the wheezes aren't completely better. But, if it's all clear, what do you say, Sally?'

'Well, it certainly sounds tempting. Would you want me to drive, Brad, or do you have your own car?' The child giggled.

'Reckon Dad wants to go too. Please

say you'll come.'

Sally hesitated. Her good intentions were rapidly going out of the window. It seemed impossible to avoid these two males and she knew she would have a great day out with them. If Maria was keeping away from them, what harm could it do? She accepted the invitation and the plans were made.

'Shall I pack a picnic?'

'We can get nice sandwiches there. Doesn't seem worth the effort of packing up.'

'All right, but this time, it's definitely on me. Just you make sure you don't get any worse, Brad. We won't be able to do anything if you're poorly.'

'What's poorly?' Brad asked curiously.

'Not well.'

'Bit like being crook,' Adam supplied.

'Crook?' Sally asked.

They all giggled.

'And to think, we're all speaking English. Same only different, I guess.'

5

Sally worked hard for the rest of the week. She made a number of visits and sent information back to her boss in England. He seemed pleased with her efforts and was already suggesting her stay could be longer than initially planned.

As everything was still quite new to her, she felt happy at the thought of more time to explore the beautiful surroundings, as well as to build up the business. It was also nice to have found a friend in Adam, though the prospect of spending too much time with him still alarmed her slightly.

As for Brad, he was quite adorable and she had never shown any interest in children before so this was another scary aspect to any future friendship they might share.

Saturday was rather dull and rain

threatened. Rather than a long trip into the mountains, they decided to visit one of the areas around Mount Tarawera, the volcano that had buried a village when it erupted over a hundred years ago.

There was a visitors' centre there, where they could shelter if the rain came down.

'When it rains here, it certainly knows how to wet a person,' Adam told her.

She was fascinated by the old buildings that had been dug out of the mud that once engulfed the village and she learned something of the history of an area that was totally moulded by its environment.

'Somehow, you get a feeling that you can't totally rely on this place. It's magnificently beautiful, but it's somehow always in charge. You can look at something and wonder if it will still be there in a few years. England is much more permanent in a way.'

'I guess I know what you mean.

Some of the thermal areas change each year. New lakes form and places that had safe paths have lost them as they collapse into a new little crater. We must take you to see the boiling mud next.'

'Yes, please,' shrieked Brad. 'It's so gross. You'll love it.' Sally laughed and held tight to his little hand when it was pushed into hers. She felt strangely moved by the feel of it.

It had been another lovely day spent together and over a shared pizza in the evening, Sally tried to ask as casually as she could, a bit more about the situation with Maria. Adam glanced at his son and shook his head very slightly. Clearly he was unwilling to talk in front of Brad. The little boy was almost falling asleep and was ready for bed.

'I think I should go too,' Sally said. 'I need to call my parents and well, I'm pretty tired too. It's been really good. Thank you for sharing your precious Saturday with me.'

'Maybe we could have dinner one

evening?' Adam asked. 'Just the two of us? There's lots to talk about.'

She hesitated. She was anxious to have a chance to talk to this intriguing man and find out what made him tick. She felt slightly scared by the depth of feeling she was experiencing for someone who was so recent an acquaintance.

'OK. That'd be nice. Give me a call.'

'Great. Tuesday or Wednesday would be good for me. Would that work for you?'

'I think so. I do have to make a longer trip quite soon but nothing's fixed yet. Say Tuesday, but I'll need to confirm it when I look at my schedule.' She hated herself for sounding so formal and busy but she knew she was still fighting an inner conflict.

Though she had called to confirm their dinner . . . was it actually a date? Sally was still filled with doubts about the wisdom of such an outing. She still took care with her choice of clothes, wanting to look smart, but trying to keep it fairly casual.

The blue silk shirt she chose, brought out the colour of her eyes. She hesitated about the gold chain she'd inherited from her granny and decided it might look as if she was dressing up too much.

Instead, she wore the pendant she had bought at the weekend when they'd all been out together. It was made of paua shell, the local shell that came in shades of turquoise. It wasn't expensive, but she was fascinated by the range of colours and it looked good with her shirt. She had just finished when her doorbell rang.

'Hi. You look nice.' Adam sounded casual and she smiled back, wondering if this evening was going to answer any of the questions that teemed through her mind. 'I thought we'd drive out along the coast a little way. There are some nice bars and restaurants near the beach. Quite lively at this time of year.'

'Fine,' she agreed, though a lively bar was hardly going to provide much opportunity for the talk she was hoping for.

It was a happy evening. He made her laugh most of the time as he recounted his tales of computer disasters he'd been called out to fix.

'One of the worst was the child who'd carefully poured his orange juice all over the keyboard to see where it went to. Fortunately, keyboards aren't that expensive and it hadn't got into the computer itself.'

All too soon, it was getting late and she still hadn't broached the subject of the state of his marriage. She took a deep breath and asked him outright.

'So, don't you and Maria see much of each other? Are you actually separated?'

'Difficult. I try to stay on good terms for Brad's sake. Now, if you're done, shall we leave?'

'Sure. Sorry if you don't want to talk about it, but I need to know where I am.'

'I don't want to talk. As for you, I

enjoy being with you and so does Brad. I'll pay up and we'll go now.'

He strode away and she could do nothing more than gather her things together and follow him. Clearly, she had touched on delicate ground and probably upset him. This was going nowhere and she was wasting her time even thinking about Adam and his son in anything more than casual terms.

They drove home in almost total silence. She had commented about the lights reflected in the water and how nice it was to be out without a coat in the late evening. He'd responded, but offered no conversation of his own. She knew she'd blown the whole thing and it was time to move on. She thanked him for a pleasant evening and waved as he drove away.

Sally tried hard to immerse herself in her work and made herself go out as much as she could. But it wasn't the same. She had been with Rob for most of her adult life and travelling round to look at the sights wasn't much fun on her own.

After almost two months time spent in the country, she had covered many miles and was gradually building up her contacts. She went out for occasional meals with one or two of the clients she had met, but it was mainly polite business socialising and nothing more.

She had neither seen or heard anything more from Adam and apart from a polite thank you note for the dinner, she had made no more contact with him. Clearly, she had frightened him off with too many questions. Despite their short acquaintance, she'd been attracted to him and she missed him. Her pride was preventing her from calling him again.

During her weekly phone call home to her parents at the weekend, she got a huge surprise.

'Your father thinks we should come over and see you. What do you think?'

'Oh, Mummy, that's terrific. I'm delighted. How soon can you be here?'

'Well, we've looked into flights and it seems there's a special offer if we book right away. We could be with you in the next two weeks. Can you cope with that?'

'Cope with it? It's the best news I've had for ages. I never thought you'd actually do it. I'm planning a trip to South Island soon, so you could come too and we can combine business and pleasure.'

They chatted on, each of them getting more excited at the prospect. It was a huge adventure for her mother who had previously made only short holiday trips to the Continent throughout her life. They agreed to speak again later in the week when the tickets were finalised. She went into overdrive, planning how she could move things around in the flat and working out places to go.

If she organised her visits for mornings, she could be free for most of the rest of the days so she could spend time with her parents. She almost managed to forget Adam in her frenzy of organising.

★ ★ ★

When her parents had recovered from their long flight, they were ready to explore and just as Sally had, immediately fell in love with the country. After a few days in the little town, they began their expedition to South Island. It was great to have someone to share the driving on the long trip.

'I didn't think I'd take to driving in a foreign country, but it's no different really,' her father announced.

'Course it isn't. We drive on the left here same as at home and the roads are less crowded once you're out of the city.'

They had a perfect crossing on the Inter Island ferry and watched for signs of dolphins as they sailed down the picturesque fiords. They had a busy time in the main wine producing areas and visited a number of vineyards, each one offering wine tastings.

Taking turns at driving became essential to remain within the law!

'I'm sorry we can't spend longer,' she said after a week, 'but I have to get back to the office. I have spoken to my boss, but he needs me back there.'

'It's been wonderful, darling,' her mother said with great enthusiasm. 'But it will be nice to stay in the same place for more than one night at a time. I can't believe we've only got a few more days and it's time to go back home.'

'It's gone very quickly. But at least you now know where I am and what I'm doing.'

'I can imagine you when you answer the phone, sitting on your sofa with that gorgeous sea view in front of you. Makes you seem less far away.'

They arrived home late in the afternoon, tired and hungry.

'I'll go for a takeaway,' Sally offered.

'I'll go,' said her father. 'Then you can answer your messages. That light on your answering machine looks as if it might take off at any moment.' She nodded her thanks and he left.

She pressed the play button.

'You have twenty-seven messages,' the electronic voice told her.

'Heavens,' her mother said. 'You're popular with someone.'

She began to play them.

'Sally? It's Adam. Look, I know I haven't been in touch for some time, but I need to speak to you urgently. Call me back. Please.'

The next fifteen said more or less the same thing, with an increasing sense of anxiety. Number fifteen held a note of anger.

'Look, I wouldn't ask, but it's Brad. We really need you. Please forget about us and for his sake, please will you at least reply. It's now Thursday. Nine p.m.'

There were a couple more messages from people trying to sell something and then more from Adam. She smiled apologetically at her mother and dialled his number.

'Hi. It's me. I've only just got back from a trip to South Island. What's the problem?'

'Oh, thank heavens! I thought you were deliberately avoiding speaking to me. It's Brad. He's had a really bad attack of asthma and he's in hospital. He's really stressed and anxious. He keeps asking for you. You know how much he enjoys your company and frankly, we're desperate to motivate him. Please say you'll come and visit him. He's in the local hospital.'

'Oh, Adam, of course I will. Poor little Brad. But it's rather late now and I've got my parents over on a visit. I'll go first thing tomorrow, if that's OK. We've only just got back and I'm shattered and starving.'

'Thank you, Sally. I'm really grateful. Can I pick you up first thing? The sooner we can do this, the better.'

'OK then. I'll see you around nine?' She put the phone down, looking anxious.

'So, who's this Adam?'

'Oh, just the man who looks after my computer. Business acquaintance.'

'And Brad? I think you mentioned him too.'

She spent an awkward few minutes trying to explain and trying to say that she knew the child through babysitting him a couple of times. It was almost true. She was spared further probing when her father returned with hot pizzas for them all.

'So what did he mean by the 'forget about us', your Adam mentioned?' Her mother asked when they had finished. Sally gave a small sigh.

'He isn't my Adam. He's married, but I think he's separated. I guess he's referring to the fact that last time we met, I was probably asking too many questions.'

'I see. Well, no doubt you'll explain yourself when you're ready.'

'I don't know how you feel, but I could do with an early night. I'm shattered.' Sally yawned as she spoke.

'And you'll want an early start

tomorrow. With Adam calling round for you. Do we get to meet him?'

'Oh, Mum, please don't pester me. We're going to the hospital to see his little boy, not on some date.'

'But you obviously know the little boy well enough for him to ask to see you.'

'I can't explain why he wants to see me, but if it helps him to get better, that's fine by me.'

'Have you got something to take for him? A little book or something?'

'Nothing at all. I wonder if there's a shop at the hospital or somewhere we can call on the way. I don't have anything here I could take and it's much too late to go searching for a shop that's open. Too bad. He'll have to make do with me. Shall I use the bathroom first?'

Despite feeling exhausted, Sally slept fitfully. She tossed around on the sofa bed and hoped the creaks didn't wake her parents in the next room. She felt concerned about Brad and wondered why she was the one to be summoned to his bedside.

Where was his mother in all this? Suppose she also went to the hospital and they actually met? It could cause all sorts of problems. It was all futile speculation but nevertheless, it managed to keep her awake for much of the night. It was seven o'clock when her mother crept through the room to go into the kitchen.

'Sorry, love. I didn't mean to wake you. Your father and I were longing for a cuppa. Can I get you one?'

'It's all right. Help yourself. I think I could do with coffee.' Her parents always liked tea first thing, but after her restless night, she needed a caffeine kick to get her going. She felt a mixture of nervous, excited and of course, concern for Brad. She hoped it would be a typical child thing . . . really sick one minute and fine and raring to go the next.

When her doorbell rang, she grabbed her bag and ran down the stairs. She called back, 'You can take the car, Dad. I've left the keys on the side. Why don't you come to the office around lunchtime? I'll meet you there.'

At least she'd avoided having to introduce Adam to her parents and give her mother time to speculate.

'How is he? Really?' she asked immediately.

'His breathing seems better, but he's so listless and doesn't seem to show interest in anything. He was asking for you as soon as he was over the worst.'

'Can't think why. Sorry I couldn't respond sooner, but I was away, as I said.'

'How long are your parents here?'

'They go back in a few days. Thursday, I think it is.'

'Sorry to drag you away from them.'

'No problem. I've been able to leave them the car and if you drop me back at the office, they'll come there and we can have lunch together, at least.'

'So I can't persuade you to join me?

As a thank you for your time this morning?'

'I'll give it a miss this time, thanks. It would be embarrassment all round if you joined me and the parents. My mother seems to think I'm on the shelf and if a halfway suitable male appears on the scene, she's looking at wedding hats.'

'Hardly on the shelf. Haven't you left a boyfriend languishing behind?'

'Well, I did have a fiancé, but he didn't like the idea of my travelling anywhere without him and so we finished.' She touched her ring finger, feeling the slight groove that was still there after so many months of wearing an engagement ring. She realised she'd scarcely given Rob a thought since she'd been in New Zealand. That must mean something, she told herself.

'So am I halfway suitable? As a male?' She ignored him as she flushed furiously. 'Here we are. I'll park over here and then it's not too far to walk. Hope this is going to do the trick.'

They went into the cheerful little ward where several children were playing with some games on one side, while others were lying in their beds. She saw Brad, pale and listless lying back against the pale green pillows.

'Hi, Brad. What's all this? Fancy getting yourself so poorly that you have to stay in hospital.'

'Am I really poorly?' he said imitating her accent. 'I didn't think you were going to come and see me. Dad said he'd tried to call you, but you didn't answer.'

'I was away, Brad. I've been to South Island and my mum and dad are over here staying with me so it's been quite a busy few days.'

'Do their noses turn blue and have they got ten arms and legs hidden under their jackets?' he asked with a big grin.

'Only when they're very cross.' She laughed. 'It's good to see you laughing. I was worried about you.'

'Were you really?'

'Course I was. I only got home last night and here I am right away.'

They all chatted for a while and Brad was visibly brighter. He began to show interest in some of the things the other children were playing with.

'Do you think I might be allowed to play with some of those toys?' he asked.

'I expect so,' Adam told him. 'You just have to be careful not to run around and get the wheezes worse. But you could probably sit at that big table and play.'

The little boy pushed the covers back and waited to be lifted down. There were bars at the side of his bed to prevent him falling out and he held his arms out. One of the nurses came over.

'You're pleased to see your mummy, aren't you?' She turned to Sally. 'This is the first time he's shown any interest in getting out of bed. I expect you've been busy?'

'I'm er . . . I'm not his mummy. I'm just a friend and I've been away on business.'

'Oh, I'm sorry.' She lifted Brad down and looked embarrassed. 'Take care now. No running around until you're lots better.'

He smiled at them and took Sally's hand.

'Will you come and look at the cars with me?' She followed him across the room and sat him down. Adam watched from the bedside and gave a wry grin. However much he had resolved not to be involved with this English girl, his son wasn't going to allow it. Blast Maria and her threats. She was living the life she wanted and he'd been left looking after their child with threats hanging over him if he as much as looked at anyone else. How had he ever come to marry a selfish woman like her?

Brad hadn't once asked to see his mother and here was Sally, someone he'd met only a few times, adopting the role she should have been filling. Something had to be done about it, for sure.

'I'm going to have to leave you now, Brad,' Sally was saying. 'I have to go to work, but I'll come back again really soon. You get yourself better as soon as you can and maybe we can have another day out?'

'Yes pleeeeeease,' he said happily. 'Daddy said you might not want to see us again, but he was wrong, wasn't he? I wish you could be my mummy instead of Maria. You could be, you know,' he added earnestly. 'That nurse thought you were her, didn't she?'

'Maybe,' Sally replied uncomfortably. 'Take care and see you soon.' She gave him a hug and Adam did the same.

'Bye.' He put down the car and waved his little hand as they left.

'Thanks so much. It was like a miracle. He simply refused to get out of bed and if they lifted him out he screamed and just made himself worse.'

'Hope it helped. Can't think why I'm anyone so special.'

'I'm sorry about the mummy thing. Hope you didn't mind too much.'

'Actually, why isn't Maria here? I'd have thought she'd want to see him and even help out.'

'She's organising some big conference. She has phoned a couple of times.' He sounded defensive.

'I'm sorry, but surely her own son comes before some work event? What's the matter with her?'

'It's complicated.'

'Complicated how?'

'Oh heck. I might as well tell you. I've asked her for a divorce.'

'I see. Well, it's obvious something's not right between you, but how does that stop her coming to visit her child in hospital?'

Adam sighed and suggested they should have a coffee.

'I'll make some at the office. I really need to be there. If you don't mind stopping off for some milk on the way?'

She glanced at him as he drove and saw the worry lines around his eyes were growing deeper. He was clearly under some stress and she didn't want to make things worse by probing.

On the other hand, she really did need to know the situation and how it might affect her. Divorce? She sighed. What would her mother say? How did she feel about it, herself? Adam stopped the car near to a convenience store and leapt out to collect some milk. She stared through the window as he returned. He was such a nice person. It was a great pity that there were so many complications.

'So, penny for 'em? You've been silent ever since we left the hospital. Don't you want to be seen with a potential divorcee?'

'It's complicated.'

'That was my line. OK. Go and put that kettle on and we'll talk a while.'

The office smelt stuffy after her absence and she opened the windows. The message machine on the phone was flashing furiously. Adam plugged in her computer and switched it on.

'Thought I'd check all was well after your absence. Easier than having to come back if there's something not working.' She nodded.

'All right then. Tell me about your complicated life,' Sally instructed.

'Maria used to work at the local hospital and all was well until she decided to apply for a job in Auckland. She's a clever woman and of course, was offered the job.

'I was sort of playing the role of house husband and mostly looked after Brad myself. I was building up my computer consultancy business and managed to fit this in nicely with the childcare. I could go out in the evenings if necessary. But that wasn't good enough for Maria.

'When she got the job, the plan was that she would look around for somewhere for us to live. She chose a rather flashy apartment in a tall block. Totally unsuitable for a child. She refused to consider anything else and I refused to move. Since then, she's visited Brad once and I took him up there for a couple of weekends. Total disaster. He hated it. Nowhere to play and the traffic fumes did him no good.'

'But I thought Auckland was a beautiful, clean city? All that water and boats everywhere.'

'Oh it is. Don't get me wrong. But it is still a busy city and walking along the roads at Brad height, you can pick up the fumes.'

'But I thought she . . . Maria, was something medical? Surely she would have been aware of all that?'

'You must realise that Maria is a single minded woman. She's ambitious and successful. I'm her first big mistake. Brad's her second. There's no real place for either of us in her plans. So, we come to the divorce.'

'I'd have thought it's exactly what she wanted. Where's the problem?'

'Divorcees are frowned upon in her circle. She plays the role of the poor woman working to support her family and no-good husband.'

'Maybe the law's different over here. I should have thought you had good grounds because of the separation.'

'She's a law to herself. Says that if I go ahead, she'll contest it and demand custody of Brad. I refuse to let him be a pawn in all of this. He knows nothing about it incidentally so keep it to yourself.'

'Of course. What a mess. But what on earth would she do if she had custody?'

'Lord knows. Poor kid scarcely knows her and would be devastated if he had to live with her. She seems to think I should live a celibate life, dedicated solely to Brad. If she ever heard I was seeing someone else, that would be it. I simply don't know how I came to marry someone so selfish. But, I did. It means I daren't risk being seen with you any more. Not for a while, anyhow.'

'And does Maria live a celibate life?'

'I doubt it. Knowing her.'

'But Adam, it's all ridiculous. I'm not saying we're exactly seeing each other, but why shouldn't you go out occasionally if you want to?'

'I daren't risk losing Brad. As you

say, it's a ridiculous situation, but until negotiations are underway and less delicate, I'll have to stay away from you. There's no alternative.'

Sally felt tears threatening and swallowed the last of her coffee. There was a lump in her throat and her voice croaked slightly.

'I'd better get on with some work. I have masses to catch upon. Reports to write.'

'I'm sorry, Sally. Thank you so much for coming to the hospital with me.'

'That's it then? I can't keep my promise to visit Brad again. And by the time you are free to see me again, I shall probably be packing up to leave. Thanks anyway. It's been nice knowing you. You should go now. Someone might see you.'

'Sally . . . don't let's part like this. I'll call you.' He looked so distressed that she wanted to hold him in her arms and hug him better. But she made herself look away and pressed the button on her phone to retrieve her messages.

He left the office and went out to his car. She watched as he drove away and realised the voice speaking on her answering machine was Adam himself. He'd left several messages asking her to call him, just as he had at her home. With eyes streaming with tears, she erased his messages and set about dealing with all the business matters.

6

Sally busied herself with her e-mails and writing up reports from her visits. She tried to engross herself with the tasks, but her mind was filled with the picture of the little boy in his hospital bed and the grin he gave her when she visited him. Adam also featured strongly in her thoughts and she finally admitted to herself that in any other circumstances, she might think she was falling in love with him. But that was not even a distant possibility and she must remove him from her thoughts. The door opened and her mother breezed in.

'Only us, darling. You ready for lunch? Dad's left the engine running. We thought it would be nice if we went down near the harbour. What do you think?'

'Oh, Mum. I'm snowed under here,'

Sally said quickly. 'I'm really sorry, but I really need to work through.' She hoped her parents might take the hint and leave her alone to lick her wounds.

'Nonsense, dear. We want to hear all about your visit to the hospital. How's the little boy? And besides, you need to eat properly. You're looking quite peaky.'

Sally sighed and switched off her computer. She put the answering machine on again and picked up her bag.

'OK. You win.' She knew that resistance was futile when her mother wanted her to do something. They would be leaving for home in a few days and after that, Sally would have more than enough time on her hands to do all the work anyone could want of her.

They drove along the coast for a few kilometres and stopped at a small seaside café. It was simple food and as usual in the area, freshly prepared.

'Makes a nice change to have sandwiches served on a plate instead of out of a nasty plastic box. They seem to taste much better don't you think?' her mother babbled on. She kept scrutinising Sally sharply, looking for a clue as to why her previously happy daughter suddenly looked so drawn. 'Are you sure the little boy was on the mend?' she asked once more.

'Yes, thanks. He was much better. I left him playing happily with the other children.'

'Did you actually say what the relationship is?'

'There's no relationship, Mum. Adam, Brad's father, is the man who looks after the computer. He had to bring Brad to the office with him one day and then left him with me when he went to buy a new part. Seems Brad liked me and wanted me to visit him.'

'But you've never had much to do with children. I don't understand why he was asking for you? Where's his mother in all this?'

'It's complicated. She works in Auckland,' she explained wearily. 'Now, can we please drop the subject? What have you been doing with your morning?'

They chatted about the shops they'd visited and other inconsequential matters. Sally was anxious to avoid any more interrogation and wanted to get back to work.

'Why don't you go and visit the buried village? It's beautiful country around there and you'd enjoy it. I'm sorry, but I really do have to get back to work now.' She explained how to get there and even admitted to visiting the site herself but managed to keep Adam and Brad out of the scenario.

They left her at her office and drove away. She tried to immerse herself in her work once more, but the face of the little boy in his hospital bed kept coming back to her.

Adam was never far away from her thoughts either and she thought about the unfairness of it all.

After supper, her father went for a stroll along the beach, leaving Sally to the mercy of her mother.

'You're in love with this Adam, aren't you, dear?' her mother said, as casually as she might have admired a dress she was wearing.

'Of course I'm not. He's very nice, but love? Huh. No way. Besides, I hardly know him.'

'You don't fool me. I'd have liked to meet him. Just so I could form an opinion. But, I understand there are difficulties. I'm right about him though, aren't I?'

'No, Mum. Stop speculating and let me get on with the dishes. You bribed Dad to go out didn't you?'

'I just thought it might be better to have a talk on our own. I don't like you to be unhappy. In fact, what you really ought to do is pack up right now and come back with us. I'm sure Gary would understand. It's been a wonderful experience for you, but you can't stay here on your own. Knowing no-one. Involved with a married man and a potentially messy divorce.'

'Mum. You've been reading too many novels. I'm not involved with Adam. We've been out a couple of times and his kid seems to like me. That's it. End of story. And no. No way am I going home with you. I'm going to see this job through and somehow, I shall separate Adam from any part of my life. Even if it means finding a new computer expert.'

Her mother sighed and began to run water into the washing up bowl. Sally picked up the tea cloth to wipe up and tried to smile. It would have been comforting to go back to England and the safety of her old home, but it would still be going back. Rob would still be around and everything would be just as it was before. Her mother was of course quite right. She had fallen in love with Adam and she would simply need to avoid him. That was surely not too difficult with a whole new country to explore?

All too soon, she was driving her parents to Auckland and the airport.

They were all slightly tearful as they parted, but they promised to come back for another visit if Sally didn't go home.

'Try to be happy, darling,' her mother urged. 'It will all work out in the end.'

She waved as they went through security and hid her tears behind a smile.

'Come back soon,' she called as they disappeared from her sight. There was no point hanging around to watch the flight leave and she began the long drive back. She wondered if Brad had been released from the hospital and what they were doing. Nothing to do with her. Now she needed to knuckle down to her work and make Gary, her boss back in England, very proud of her and what she might achieve.

For the next month, there was little in her life apart from work. She met a number of new people through work and even made the odd friend or two, but however much she tried to push away her thoughts of Adam, he kept appearing in her thoughts.

She was packing up at the end of the week, wondering how she might spend the weekend when the office door opened. She glanced around and stopped in her tracks. She stared at the man in front of her, quite convinced she was dreaming.

'How . . . what on earth are you doing here?'

'Hello, Sally. How are you?'

'But . . . Rob? How did you . . . I mean . . . why . . . ' she knew she was blabbering, but it was such a shock.

'Your mum met me at the supermarket. She said what a wonderful time they'd had over here with you and thought you might even be just a little pleased to see me. I hope you are.'

'I'm not sure why you're here, but well, I suppose it's nice to see you. Though please don't think we can ever get back together. If that's your scheme, forget it and fly right back again now.'

'Sally . . . we've known each other since we were kids. If we can't be any more to each other, surely we're still good friends?'

'I guess. Where are you staying?'

'I haven't booked anything. Your mother said you have a couch. I wondered if I could crash with you for a while?'

'I'm not sure it's a good idea.'

'Oh, I'm sorry. I never thought. Maybe you've got someone else in your life. Only your mother said you'd had a disappointment . . . well, met someone who . . . '

'My mother had no right to say anything. To you of all people. I can't believe she'd do such a thing.'

'Please, Sally. Let's be friends. I'm not asking any more of you. Let's just spend a little time together and have a bit of a holiday.'

'I'm working, in case you hadn't noticed. I spent time with my parents and really can't take anymore time off.'

They talked for a while. Bickered a little. Finally, Sally gave in and agreed that Rob could come to stay with her. It was so strange seeing him again. So familiar yet almost a stranger in these new surroundings. It was interesting to realise that she felt nothing more than an old, perhaps slightly tired, friendship towards him. He insisted on taking her out for dinner and over the meal, he became a little less cautious. As they were using her car, he perhaps drank a little more wine than was sensible.

'Sally, I still love you. Can't we try again? You could come back with me and we could take up our plans where we left off. I've got a good job and we could afford to buy a house . . . near to your parents if you like.'

'Rob, please stop right there. I can't go back. Not until I've made a go of things here. And in any case, I don't love you. Not any more.'

'If you ever did truly love me,' he said bitterly. 'We took it all for granted. You just thought it was convenient to have me near home didn't you?'

'Don't be silly, Rob. Yes, we certainly did grow up together and became more than friends, probably because we saw each other every day. It was sort of expected by everyone that we'd get together long term. But I'm not sure if it really was love or not. If one can ever truly define love. Of course, I'm fond of you. We have so much history. But that's it. Nothing more and you won't make me change my mind. If that's your reason for staying, forget it.' He stared at her for a moment.

'Remember that first time we went out together? Properly, I mean.'

'Of course I do. I was quite shocked when you turned up in a posh T-shirt and carrying chocolates. How old were we? Fourteen or something?'

'About that. Ah well. Happy times. Now, what are we going to do this weekend? What is there to do and see around here?'

Sally had been planning a quiet weekend, catching up on chores and maybe spending some time at the beach after the inevitable shopping. She suggested a few of the local places to visit and realised she was practically becoming a tour guide. Fascinating though it all was, it might become less interesting after several visits with her various guests.

Maybe she should suggest he should hire a car and go out on his own when she was back at work on Monday. But, after he had gone to the effort and expense of flying out here, she ought to spend a bit of time with him even if only for old times' sake.

They spent Saturday seeing the local sights and planned a longer trip for Sunday morning. She was stuffing her swimming togs into a bag when the doorbell rang.

'I'll get it,' Rob called and before she could protest he'd opened the door.

'Oh,' said a startled Adam. 'I . . . I er was looking for Sally.'

'Sal,' Rob shouted. 'Someone wants you, darling.'

'Oh Adam. How are you?' She felt her knees going weak and her heart began to pound at the sight of him.

'Please, come in, how's Brad?'

'It's all right. You're obviously busy,' he said, his head inclining towards Rob who leaned on the door post looking slightly amused.

'No, I'm not. This is Rob. A friend from the UK visiting New Zealand for the first time. Is there a problem?'

'Well, yes. I wouldn't have bothered you, but I'm a bit desperate. I have to meet Maria and well, as you know, things are never easy. I didn't want Brad to have to witness our rows yet again. But I wouldn't dream of interrupting anything for you. It's fine. I shouldn't be here anyhow. Sorry to intrude. I was quite wrong to come here.'

'Adam. Please wait.'

He walked away with a casual wave over his shoulder. Clearly, he had misinterpreted the situation and thanks to Rob, she had probably lost any chance of seeing Adam or Brad again. He must think she was a very fast worker to have someone staying with her so soon.

'Thanks a bunch,' she snapped at Rob. 'What was the *darling* all about?'

'Couldn't resist. Some problem? Was he anyone special?'

'Probably not any more. It's complicated.' She felt tears burning. Why did it have to happen now? She would have given anything to have Brad stay with her for the day and maybe have dinner with Adam during the evening. There might have been a future for them after all. Pipe dreams. All pipe dreams.

'Are you ready to go then?' Rob asked cheerfully.

'I suppose so.' What she would really like to do was sit quietly and brood over lost opportunities, but that was impossible and probably not very sensible either. 'I'll get my stuff and we can go.'

It was not the most successful of days. Rob began to snipe at her for being so quiet and then became apologetic because he'd been cross. He persisted in asking her about Adam and finally, she gave him the gist of the story. He listened carefully and came to the conclusion that she was seeking pie in the sky.

Her concentration was shattered and she managed to dent the car when she was negotiating round a load of rocks on a narrow track. The final straw to a disappointing day, came when they got soaked during a sudden downpour.

'I'm sick of today,' Sally grumbled. 'Let's go back to my apartment and get dry again. Sorry I'm grumpy, but I've got a lot on my mind.'

'I'll cook supper,' Rob offered. 'You have a nice long bath and relax. I'll pour you a glass of wine and you can soak in lots of bubbles or whatever you need to get rid of your stress.'

'Thanks,' she replied with no enthusiasm. She should try to make an effort but she felt sick with disappointment.

When she came from the bathroom, Rob had set the table with candles and had even produced some flowers from somewhere or other. He opened champagne and poured them a glass each.

'Sorry they're the wrong glasses, but

I couldn't find proper champagne flutes.'

'Don't have such things anyhow. This is very nice. Where did you get this from?' She nodded at the bottle.

'Bought it on the flight over. I slipped it into the fridge this morning so it would be chilled and ready, sit down and I'll bring in the starter.'

He had produced a wonderful meal from the ingredients he must have organised at some point. Smoked salmon, followed by a delicious chicken dish with fresh vegetables. Dessert was fresh strawberries and cream and there was coffee and brandy to round it off.

'Oh, I nearly forgot.' He produced a box of chocolates, exactly the same as the ones he had given her on their first date all those years ago.

'Oh Rob, I don't deserve all this. Thank you.'

'Open the chocolates.'

Sally lifted the lid and there, in the middle of the box was her engagement ring. The same ring she had given back to him when she told him of her intentions of making this trip to New Zealand.

'Will you marry me, Sally? This is your ring and nobody else's.'

'Rob I told you. It's over for me. I can't marry you and if this meal was supposed to soften me up, it didn't work. I'm so sorry.'

Choking back her tears, she rushed out of the room. She didn't want to hurt him any more than she had already and he was making it so difficult for both of them. He was a thoroughly nice man, but she didn't love him and however nice a person was, that was not sufficient grounds for a happy future. She hugged her pillow to her chest and allowed the tears to roll down her cheeks.

She could hear Rob crashing around in the next room. The dishes were clattering, presumably as he was clearing up. She thought about it. Could she even consider returning to England and even marrying him? She had told him several times during the last couple of days, but her life here had not been one hundred percent happy.

How long was it now? Only around four months and she had met someone she thought she loved after very little time spent together. She had known Rob for years and was turning him down again. Why?

The flat was suddenly silent. She could hear no movements and wondered what Rob was doing. She went into the sitting room but it was empty. So was the kitchen. The dishes had been stacked in the sink but there was no sign of Rob himself. She looked in the cupboard where his holdall had been stored. It was still there and his shaving things were still in the bathroom. He'd obviously gone for a walk, she assumed.

She ran water into the sink and began to clean the dishes. Rob was a good cook, but he did seem to need to use every last pot, pan and dish to achieve his aims. She put everything away and wondered when he would be back.

Even more, she wondered what she was going to say to him. Undoubtedly, she was very fond of him. They had too much history for her to feel any other way. Maybe she should reconsider and even think of returning. Any future she might have had with Adam was now ruined and she doubted she would ever again see either him or his little boy.

Her brain reeling, she went to bed. Coward she was, it meant she didn't have to face Rob again. He had a key to her flat and could let himself in.

Exhausted, Sally slept deeply despite her troubles and when she got up the next day, Rob was making coffee and his holdall stood on the sofa, packed and ready to go.

'Sal . . . please think very hard what you are doing. You will end up lonely and miserable if you stay here, dreaming of a future with someone who clearly can't or won't commit. Come back with me.'

'I can't, Rob. But I'll think about it. I promise. I have to make this job work and I'm committed to six months minimum. I . . . er . . . gather you're leaving?'

'Thought it best. I'm flying down to South Island. Got a flight from the local airport. I'll hire a car and see the sights. I have almost a couple of weeks of my holiday left so might as well make the most of it. May not be the way I'd hoped to spend the time, but that's life. May catch you on my way back?'

'Yes. Yes of course. Good idea. I can drive you back to Auckland if you need me to.' She felt such a huge overwhelming relief that he was leaving, she even offered to take him to the local airport right away.

'Keen to be rid of me?' he teased.

'Don't be silly. I'm just a bit tense.'

'Come here. Give me a hug.'

She did so and realised it was like hugging an old friend or family. There was simply nothing romantic in the gesture and she felt no thrill of excitement.

She drove him to the airport and stopped outside the terminal.

'Goodbye, and thanks for coming so far to see me. I'm sorry things didn't work out the way you hoped.' She smiled as she spoke, but he turned on her angrily.

'You should come down to earth. See reality and not try living in some futile dream. You have to accept that you can't have Adam. Just be sensible and come back with me. You have almost two weeks to come to your senses. Thanks for the lift.' He got out of the car, snatched his bag from the rear seat and stormed away. Sally grimaced and waved to his retreating figure.

'Oh, Adam, have I really lost you too?' she muttered aloud.

7

Sally threw herself into work for the next few days. It was easy to lose herself in the thrill of finding new contacts and dealing with growers all over this exciting country. She made a trip to the west coast, stopping on her way to explore even more amazing places. She came to the conclusion that New Zealand had more geographical oddities than anywhere else she knew of. She did lose count of the number of times her hand reached for the phone to call Adam. Desperately, she wanted to explain to him the true situation that existed with Rob and tell him that nothing was as it looked. But each time, she resisted her impulse.

'Morning,' the postman called as he came into the office to deliver her mail. 'Nice to see you back. Been off travelling again?'

'Just a quick trip to the west coast. Here for a few days now. Thanks for the mail.'

He left her with a heap of envelopes, most of which seemed to be flyers or junk mail. She put it into her recycling box unopened, thinking the problems of waste paper were no better over here. She looked at a couple of bills and some invoices and slit open one final typewritten envelope. She could scarcely believe what she was reading.

Leave him alone.

You're breaking up a happy family with your selfishness.

Don't you have any morals, having an affair with a married man?

How many men do you need in your life?

Do you have to try and steal someone else's child?

Can't you have one of your own?

You're ruining both their lives.

It was naturally unsigned, but the message was clear. Angrily, she screwed it up and threw it in the bin. It had left a nasty taste and she found concentration difficult. The next morning another letter arrived, saying much the same thing again, but with even nastier words. A third letter was the final straw. Who could be sending them and what on earth did they think was going on? She hadn't even seen Adam for weeks and certainly had nothing to be ashamed of.

The postmarks were all damaged and gave no clear indication where they were posted. The only person she could think of who might have sent it, was Maria. But surely, she would never have stooped so low? Then she was struck by another thought. Could it have been Rob? But that was also out of character. She was very upset and then became angry. How dare someone send these letters to her?

It was hateful, unfounded and cowardly. This time she did dial Adam's number.

'Adam? It's Sally. I need to talk to you. Something's happened.'

'Are you all right? You're not ill, are you?' He sounded most concerned and drove to her office right away.

Silently, he read the two letters she had kept.

'Have you got the envelopes?' She nodded and handed them over. 'Nothing to identify them. And the postmark's blurred. That's strange in itself. Can't think why anyone would be so nasty and it's all unfounded anyhow. We've hardly seen each other for weeks. In any case, you clearly have someone else in your life.'

'I need to explain about Rob.'

'Of course you don't. Nothing to do with me. You have your life to live. I'll admit I was disappointed you'd found someone so soon. In other circumstances I'd had high hopes you might think of me as more than just a computer expert.'

'But I do, Adam. Very much so. It was you who backed off. And honestly, there's nothing going on with Rob. He's my ex. Came over to try and persuade me to go back to him. He's left though and I'll never go back to him.'

'I see. Oh, Sally, why does everything have to be such a mess? So complicated?'

'So, you think it could be Maria? Sending this horrible stuff to me?'

'Seems rather out of character. She's an intelligent woman and has a busy life. I don't even think she wants Brad in her life. Just doesn't want me to be happy without her.'

'Dog in the manger. But to stoop so low as to write anonymous letters. How does she know who I am? Where I work?'

'I'll go and see her as soon as I can get away. Sally, I do care you know. Very much. It's been dreadful being without you these last few weeks and then when we called at your flat and I saw your . . . what's his name? Rob . . . ?' He took her in his arms and pulled her close. Very gently, his lips brushed hers and she felt as if she were flying. She put her arms round him and kissed him back.

'We should be careful. Anyone passing could look in and see us.'

'Then someone might have grounds for the accusations.'

'Please try and sort it out, Adam. I can't cope with this.'

'I'll set out tomorrow. Brad's at school and if I set out first thing, I can be back in time for the end of the day.' He kissed the top of her head as he rushed out of her office.

Her phone rang at seven o'clock the next morning. Sleepily she lifted the receiver.

'Hello?'

'Oh, thank heavens, Sally. It's Adam. I have yet another crisis here. It's Brad. Another asthma attack and he has to go into hospital again. I daren't go to Auckland and leave him.'

'I see. I'm so sorry about Brad. Give him my love.'

'Of course. The ambulance is here. I'll be in touch soon. And throw away any more letters without opening them.

I don't want you to be upset any more. Be in touch.'

'Bye, Adam,' she muttered to the phone. She closed her eyes and remembered that tender kiss. It meant so much to know that her feelings were reciprocated, even if it was only a small gesture rather than any sort of commitment.

She heard no more for a couple of days and was on the verge of calling the hospital when Adam phoned.

'Brad's home again. Not too bad this time, but I can't send him back to school yet. I want to sort out this business once and for all. Is there any chance he could spend the day with you tomorrow? I can usually catch Maria on a Saturday, if I get there early enough.'

'If you think it's a good idea. I don't want to cause any more trouble for you.'

It was arranged that he would drop Brad at Sally's flat early the next day and drive straight on to Auckland. If he was well enough, Sally planned to take the little boy out somewhere and have some fun. Adam was very tense when he arrived and Brad looked pale and tired. She felt slightly nervous of his condition and looked at the little bag of medication in some alarm.

'Don't worry. He knows what to do and only needs a reminder of when to take his puffers. You won't forget, will you Brad?'

'Course not, Daddy. You will come back today, won't you?' He sounded anxious. All the tension could be causing his wheezes to get so bad and she was concerned about her own part in adding to it all. They waved Adam off and went back inside.

'So, what would you like to do most of all?' she asked cheerfully.

'Anything?' he asked.

'Within reason,' she conceded.

'What does that mean?'

She tried to explain, referring to his health and any other restrictions she could think of.

'Can we go on a boat? They do them

on the lakes and you can go right up to where the volcano blew up.'

Sally hesitated. Would Adam approve? Would he mind if she took him on a trip like that? She gave a shrug. He'd left his son with her and it was surely up to her what they did.

'OK,' Sally agreed. 'But you have to do everything I tell you. No messing around or anything silly.'

'Oh I wouldn't, honestly.'

They spent a happy time and Brad seemed to lose the strained look he'd had at the beginning of the day. He behaved impeccably and did everything he was told without complaint. By three o'clock, he was starting to wilt slightly and so they returned to the apartment, where he willingly took a nap. She smiled down at him as he slept. He looked so like his father.

She wondered how any mother could desert her child this way and cause such havoc in his young life. She and Adam must have been in love once. What could have gone so badly wrong?

There must be faults on both sides, even if she hadn't seen any in the man she loved. The phone rang suddenly and she quickly answered it, taking the handset into the kitchen so she didn't disturb the sleeping child.

'Hi, gorgeous. It's Rob. I shall be back in Tauranga in the morning. Wondering if you've given any more thought to my suggestion?' He sounded bright and happy.

'I'm sorry, Rob. Nothing's really changed. Do you want to call in?' she said doubtfully. She'd heard nothing from Adam and had no idea when he was going t return.

'No point. If you've decided, I'm hardly going to beg. I'm sorry of course, but that's it. Last chance?'

'I'm sorry. Look, I have to go.' She could hear Brad coughing in the next room and didn't want him to wake on his own and be frightened.

'Have you got someone else with you? Let me guess. Your married man's back on the scene. You're an idiot. It can only lead to heartache when his wife finds out.'

Sally drew in her breath sharply. What was he saying? It sounded horrible like some of the comments in the anonymous letters. Surely, they couldn't be Rob's work?

'And how will she find out?' she asked coldly.

'Someone always passes on these titbits of gossip. Makes the world go round.'

'What do you know about Adam's wife? Or anything else come to that.'

'Nothing much. Only that you seem to be making a fool of yourself and also the most colossal mistake of your life. But, that's it. No point in seeing you again. I'll give your love to your parents, shall I? Dare say I'll be seeing them in a day or two.'

'You promise you won't say anything to them?'

'We'll have to see about that. Got to go. Have a nice life.' He put the phone down and she sighed again. She really

135

hoped he wouldn't say anything to worry her parents. But, there was nothing she could do about it now. She had to consider that particular bridge was well and truly burnt.

She thought of all the happy times they had spent and felt a twinge of sadness. But she knew she had done the right thing.

She went back to Brad just as he awoke.

'I'm really hungry now,' he said happily.

'Then we'll make something to eat, shall we?'

When it got to eight o'clock and there was still no sign of his father, Brad decided he'd liked to go to sleep in Sally's bed. She began to worry slightly and hoped he hadn't had some sort of accident. She'd expected at least a call from him to say when he'd be back, but there was nothing. It was almost ten by the time she heard a car stop outside.

'Oh, thank heavens,' she said as she

opened the door. Adam came in, looking very pale and clearly under great stress. 'Brad's fast asleep in my bed. What happened?'

'The very worst. Everything's blown up in my face. Maria's agreed to a divorce all right, but at a cost. She wants a totally impossible settlement and if I continue to see you, she insists on taking Brad away from me.'

'But how on earth does she know anything about me? Not that there's anything to know.'

'We had to go to Auckland recently and called in to see her. It seems that even though it was only for an hour or so, Brad told her that Daddy had a new friend called Sally. Sally was his friend too and she wasn't really an alien but a nice lady from England. Naturally, Maria pumped him for as much information as she could get out of him and it was enough to track you down. Not too many new offices dealing with wines open so near to Tauranga, run by an English woman called Sally.'

'And did she really write those awful letters?'

'Wouldn't admit it. I'm sure it must have been though. You know, I think there's something wrong with her. Seriously. She is determined to fight for custody of Brad and yet she's never looked after him properly. Or really wanted him. I'm sure she's just trying to get back at me for having a life of my own.'

'She does sound a little unbalanced.'

'So, Sally. Can we ever have a life together?' He reached out to her.

'I'd like to think so, Adam. Truly I would.'

'There's a but coming?'

'It's all too complicated now. I think I really do love you, but there are too many imponderables. You need to get the divorce sorted out and Maria. Once that's done, let's re-think everything. I'd hate to be the cause of you being parted from Brad.'

'Give me some hope, Sally. Something to fight for.'

'I have done. I've said I love you, which is more than you've told me.'

'I fell in love with you the moment you first made me a cup of awful instant coffee. With powdered milk.' He kissed her and once more, she felt the whole world give a shudder.

'Is my daddy back yet?' Brad called from the bedroom.

'He's here, love, safe and sound,' she called back as she disengaged herself from the man she knew she loved. He held on to her hand as she went to the bedroom and she smiled back at him, gently pulling away. 'Up you get, young man. Daddy's going to take you home to your own bed now.'

'Why can't we stay here?' he asked as he rubbed sleep filled eyes.

'There isn't room, love. How are you, little lad?' Adam asked.

'OK. We had the best day. We went for a ride on the boat on the big lake in the mountains.'

'Really?' he glanced at Sally with slightly raised eyebrows.

'I hope you don't mind. It was perfectly safe and he said he'd like to go.'

'It's fine. His mother hates water and I suppose I assumed he might feel the same way. I've just never considered it. Thank you very much for looking after him, anyway.'

'It's been a pleasure. Truly. I . . . I hope things work out.' Adam nodded grimly but made no comment.

'Can we see you tomorrow?' Brad asked.

'I'm afraid I'm rather busy,' she replied uncomfortably. 'But I hope it won't be long.'

She watched them drive away and thought she caught a movement on the other side of the road. She watched for a few moments but saw nothing more. As she went inside, she saw a flash of headlights and heard a car leaving. Paranoia, she thought. It was probably just someone leaving the beach after a late walk.

A few days later, she got a phone call from Adam.

'It's happened. Maria's applied for a divorce and wants custody of Brad immediately. I'm sorry, but you have been cited.'

'Me? Why? We've done nothing.'

'Someone took pictures of me leaving your flat last Saturday night. Complete with Brad. There are others too, of you and Brad together. Seems you were followed on your trip out and her solicitor claims you are unsuitable as a child minder. Oh it's all a matter of interpretation but my solicitor says I must comply. I'm driving Brad to Auckland this morning. He wants to say goodbye to you. Can we meet somewhere?'

'I guess. But won't it make things worse?'

'It could do, but I'm past caring. Brad's very upset and doesn't want to go, of course.'

'Surely his wishes should be taken into account?'

'Eventually, yes. But I'm advised to co-operate with her demands at this stage and hopefully, it will all come right in the end.'

'I'm so sorry, Adam. Of course I'll meet you somewhere, as long as Brad isn't upset saying goodbye. How about at Bayfair? Coffee stall in the middle?'

'Good thinking. It might even look accidental. See you there in half-an-hour?'

It was a traumatic meeting. Sally felt she would always remember the sight of Brad's tear stained little face as he clung to her. Adam had almost dragged him away and only the interest in opening the package she had given to him allowed him to go.

On her way to the coffee stand, she had quickly bought a handheld, electronic game for him and the store had wrapped it in pretty paper. It was only a cheap one and she hoped it might keep him amused for a little while. Her own eyes were tear filled as she watched them leave. Adam had promised to call her later to let her know how things had gone. Somehow, she had to return to work and try to concentrate.

It was almost ten when the phone finally rang. Adam sounded exhausted and dispirited. His day had been the worst of his life, or so he said. Maria had been all sweetness and light towards Brad but pure poison to him. He'd been accused of every nasty thing she could think of, and all of it quite untrue.

'So,' he concluded, 'why don't we have dinner tomorrow night? She thinks the worst of us so why worry?'

'I'd love it, Adam, really I would. But we need time to think and let things calm down again. If you have to fight her, let's not give her any more ammunition. I simply can't believe she's doing all this just to get back at you. It's so spiteful and for someone who's a lecturer, well, it seems incredible.'

'As I said before, I think there's something wrong. I asked what was to happen to Brad while she's at work and she was very cagey. She may have lost her job. I suspect that's why she's demanding so much in terms of a divorce settlement. Please see me soon. There's so much I want to say to you and well, I just want to be with you.'

'I'll see you soon. Let the dust settle a bit.'

They said goodnight and she went to bed, hoping to get just a little sleep but expecting a restless night. When she allowed herself to think about the situation, she felt infuriated. Why should she be included in all this mess when she'd done nothing more than be a friend to Adam and Brad? Maria had a lot to answer for.

She hoped that Brad wouldn't suffer any more because of the stress. Poor little boy. He was a genuine tug of love victim, though one of the parents seemed to want to use him as a weapon rather than show genuine love and concern for him. Doubtless, he would have more asthma attacks and increase the family's stress even more.

A long, lonely week went by. Her

mother phoned at the weekend and expressed her disappointment that Sally had turned down Rob's generous offer.

'But, Mum. I don't love him. You wouldn't want me to marry someone I don't love.'

'I was so hoping you'd see reason and come back home. You belong here with us.'

'I miss you too, Mum,' she said with a knowing grin. 'But I'm making my life out here for now. Of course I'll come back one day before too long, if only for a visit.'

'I suppose you're seeing that married man again.' Disapproval poured down the phone right around the world.

'I don't know what Rob's told you. Adam and I are still in touch. But it's complicated so we're having a time out.'

'What's that supposed to mean?'

'Just leave it, Mum, please. I'll tell you when there's something to tell you. Meantime, don't let's argue. Not over the phone and at this price. I'm a big girl now, you know. I can look after myself. I had a good teacher.'

Her mother was mollified to some extent and they talked about inconsequential things for a little longer. When she put the phone down, Sally wished that everything was as simple as she had made out. She tried to pull herself together and had decided to clean the flat when the doorbell rang. Adam stood there, looking terrible.

'I had to see you. Sorry.'

'You look awful. You'd better come on.' She glanced past him into the road to see if she could spot anyone watching, but it seemed all clear. 'Sorry. I know I'm becoming paranoid.'

'I'm sorry, I've dragged you all into this. I needed to talk to you as well as to see you. Am I allowed a kiss? And a hug maybe? I so need a hug.' She laughed and put their arms round each other. She heard him draw a deep breath and he relaxed against her. The lovely warm feeling of comfort spread around her.

'I just needed to be reassured that

you are real and not some figment of my imagination.'

'I'm real enough,' she breathed. 'Can I get you some tea or coffee? Or maybe you'd like some wine?'

'Wine sounds wonderful.'

'So, what's the news? How's Brad?'

'It's driving me crazy not being with him. I've spoken briefly to him, but there's always someone listening and he seems frightened to say anything at all. I've decided to contest her for custody. I don't believe she's caring for him properly. I wanted to be sure that it isn't going to harm you in any way if I do fight hard. You're bound to be dragged into it and I'd hate it if it made things impossible for you. Job-wise, I mean as well as personally.'

'You have to fight it. Pity I didn't keep those letters after all. They might have been useful ammunition. Proved she isn't quite, well, normal.'

'You haven't had any more, have you?'

'No. Funny. I did even wonder if

they'd come from Rob at one point. Something he said. But he couldn't. Wouldn't, I'm sure. So, what's the plan?'

'I shall see my solicitor. Talk it through and see what he advises. But I'm not giving in without a fight. For Brad as well as me. It does mean that we should stay away from each other though. I don't want any more false accusations to come your way.'

'It's the right thing to do. I'd be happier with that. Much as I want you in my life, it all has to be right. My mother was disappointed that I didn't accept Rob's offer and go back to live next door to them. We had a bit of a row over it. You're known as my 'married man'. Spoken in disapproving tones of course.'

'Well, I hope I will be your own married man before too long. Your very own. Thank you for being understanding. I'd better go now or we might get spotted. I'll be in touch and hopefully, see you soon.'

'I hope so too. Good luck.'

She watched as he drove away. Why was life so complicated? It would be so much easier if we all fell in love with someone convenient and available. But it would certainly be boring.

8

Sally's boss, Gary, called her and asked her to go to Auckland for a few days. 'I'll send you the contact list and suggest you spend some time going around to meet them. Take a day or two to familiarise yourself with the city and take the clients out to a meal or two. I think it's worth doing.'

'Sure. I've been hoping to see something of the northern area too. I might take a little holiday at the same time and explore the peninsula. It's a bit like Cornwall only in reverse.'

'That's fine. We'll pay for hotels in the city and fuel of course. Enjoy. I'm pleased with progress so far. You don't intend to come back any time soon I trust?'

'No. I'm loving it here. Apart from nagging parents, I'd be happy to stay on. Can't believe it's getting on for six months already.'

'Maybe I'll take a trip out myself. See what's what.'

They chatted a little longer, but her mind was already racing. A few days spent in Auckland might be useful. She could try to find out a bit more about the mysterious Maria and even somehow, contrive to see what was happening with Brad. She picked up the directory and found a hotel. There was a website and she liked the look of it.

She glanced at a map and decided it looked convenient and booked in for three nights. She tidied her desk, set the answering machine with a new message and closed the office. Once back at the flat, she packed a few clothes, cleared the fridge and emptied the rubbish. She picked up the phone to call Adam, but thought better of it. She could organise everything she needed in Auckland and it might be better if he was unaware of her plans.

The drive north was becoming familiar after her trips to the airport.

She was unprepared for the heavy city traffic and began to think she would never find her way to the hotel or indeed, anywhere else. She seemed to get stuck on a sort of motorway and each time she left it, somehow found her way back on to it. She was usually very good at finding her way to places but now felt hot and tense and was getting desperate.

She found an exit and drove away from the main roads until she could park somewhere and study her map. Miraculously, she was in the right area for the hotel and soon found the right place. After overshooting the turning, she did a second lap with great relief and stopped in the car park. She signed in and unpacked. The shower felt wonderful and after a cup of tea and rest, she was ready to explore.

Fortunately, the hotel provided an information pack as well as directories for the city. She would find somewhere to eat, have an early night and have a good look at all the information. Once she knew where her business contacts were sited, she would see about finding Maria's apartment. Adam had mentioned it was near the hospital so that should make things easy. It was good to think she might end her speculation and see for herself how the little boy was getting on.

She had a busy time, visiting clients and invited the people at the last call of the morning to have lunch with her. They were a nice couple, a man and wife who ran their own business. They were not the biggest enterprise but she felt comfortable with them. She was able to ask about the 'must see' sights in the city and a little about the best ways to travel round. She had driven during the morning but had got lost several times and had to face the problem of parking.

'There's a good bus service and taxis aren't too expensive. By the time you've paid through the nose to park, there's probably little difference. At least the taxi drivers know where they're going.'

The wife laughed.

'How far away is the hospital?' Sally asked, trying to sound innocent.

'You're not ill are you?'

'No. I have a friend who works there. Thought I might look her up at some point.' Her fib slipped out easily.

'I see. Which department do you want? It does spread out a bit.'

'I'd need to check. Something to do with biology. Is there a medical school?'

'Oh, what's her name? We know a few people from the hospital.' Sally gave a shiver. She had already said too much.

'Gosh, is that really the time? I'm so sorry. I'll have to take my leave of you. It's been great meeting you and thanks for all the tips. I'll go and settle the bill and then I must dash. Late for an appointment,' she babbled.

'I'll get the bill. Wouldn't dream of letting you pay. It's been delightful and I'll put those papers in the post later today. When will you be back in your office?'

'That's really kind of you. I should be

back in about five days.'

She escaped and drove to her next appointment. She was somewhat early, but at least she had avoided any more awkward questions. She needed to be more careful what she said to anyone. Maybe Auckland was more of a closed community than she realised.

She glanced at her list of contacts. Just one more call and she was finished for the day. Should she try to organise someone to take out for dinner or have a quiet evening? Or should she try to find Maria's apartment and see what was going on? She decided to wait and see who the clients were and then see if she wanted to spend an evening with them.

The head of the company was a delightful middle aged man who promptly invited her to join his family for a meal at home that evening. She was very touched at his kindness and accepted. Their business was concluded quickly and he organised one of the younger staff to take her for a visit to the Sky Tower.

'Must see AKL from the Tower. Best way to get a grasp of the layout of the city and quite magnificent views. Not afraid of heights are you?'

'No, of course not. Sounds wonderful. But I ought to go back to the hotel and change before dinner.'

'Nonsense. Nothing formal at our place. You're fine as you are. You can always take a shower if you feel like you need to freshen up. My wife will be delighted to have someone to fuss over. Ah, here's Noelene. She'll take you over to the Tower. Leave your car here. Only a short walk.'

'It's really kind of you to take so much trouble.'

'Nonsense, my dear. We're always glad to see overseas visitors and we're hoping to be doing lots of business with you in the coming months.'

The Sky Tower was thrilling. She gasped at the vista of the city in front of her and all round her. It was surrounded by glimpses of blue sea with harbours and marinas and distant views of hills.

'I had no idea it was such a lovely city,' she breathed. 'I just didn't realise how much the sea is a part of it all.'

'I always think it's important to see the whole picture. Down at ground level, it seems like any other city.' Noelene was clearly proud of her birthplace. She pointed out various sights and places Sally might like to visit.

It had been a lovely day and once more Sally sent a mental thank you to her boss in England for giving her this opportunity. She finally arrived back at her hotel after eleven o'clock, well fed and feeling happy. Even the business calls had gone so well she felt relaxed and ready for a good night's sleep. Tomorrow, she would take some time to go in search of Maria's apartment and see if she could hazard any guesses about the situation with Brad and his mother. Quite what she expected to see, she had no clear idea but felt she needed to do something.

She looked in the phone book and

found an entry for M. Edwards in a block of apartments that she discovered were near the hospital. She felt certain this was the right place and drove there, parking in the large car park that said residents only. As she stopped, she saw a dark haired woman getting into a low silver sports car, driven by a blond male. He kissed her as she got into the car and they drove away.

Quickly, Sally took out her camera and managed to catch the rear of the car before it rounded the corner. She felt almost certain it was the woman in Brad's picture but in any case, she had decided to take pictures of everything she could. She went to the main entrance and saw the list of names against the various buttons. On an impulse, she pressed the one against the name of M. Edwards. A foreign sounding female voice replied.

'Yes?'

'Is Mrs Edwards in please?'

'No. She at work. Back tonight. Thank you.' The connection ended.

At least Sally knew there was someone in the flat, presumably looking after Brad. She went back to her car and sat for a little while, wondering whether she should wait or go away. She started the engine and was about to drive away when the door opened and Brad appeared with a young girl. She was grasping his hand and almost dragging him along. He was clearly angry and seemed to be trying to pull away from the girl. She pushed him into a small car and drove away.

Unable to resist following, Sally drove out of the car park, watching carefully to see the direction. She had the feeling that Brad was crying and felt her heart being ripped apart at the thought of him being so unhappy. The girl stopped outside a school and dragged Brad out of the car and in through the door. Sally grabbed her camera and took a rather blurry shot.

He was screaming, but she took no notice and pushed him inside the building. Sally felt tears burning in her eyes and as she drove away, knowing there was nothing she could do.

The au pair, as Sally assumed she must be, left him and drove away. There was no settling him in or hugs or any show of concern at all. Not knowing what else to do, she followed the girl to another car park. She stopped a few rows away and watched as the girl went into a coffee shop and sat waiting.

A man arrived and they greeted each other affectionately, kissing and hugging for a few moments. They sat together, holding hands as they ordered. Sally took some more pictures, pretending to be taking a shot of the area. She felt like she was being some kind of pathetic private investigator. There was nothing else she could do here and assumed Brad would be coming out of school at the end of the day. She would go back to the school later and sit outside and watch to see what happened.

It was a long wait, but just before three, she parked along the street and waited. Fortunately, it was a suburban area and there were no parking restrictions. At three-fifteen, the children came out of school. She saw Brad standing on the pavement, kicking his toes against the wall. He glanced up and down the street and kicked some more. He stuck a thumb in his mouth and looked dejected.

Sally was on the verge of getting out of her car when the au pair arrived, looking red faced and flustered. She flung the car door open and called to Brad immediately. They drove past her and she tried to sink back in her seat so she wasn't seen. But she caught a glimpse of Brad's face peering out of the back of the other car.

He rose and pressed himself against the rear window, as if he couldn't believe what he was seeing. He raised a hand to wave, but she started her own and drove in the other direction. Clearly though, he'd recognised her car. She knew it would be foolish to follow them home and planned to arrive there later and see if she could catch Maria

161

on her return from work.

She had a long wait. She saw the au pair's car parked and waited for the silver sports car to arrive. It was almost ten o'clock when her patience was rewarded. Maria and a man got out and with arms round each other, they went to the door where they stopped for a long kiss. Clearly, they were having some sort of relationship.

Sally snapped away with her camera and hoped that at least some of the pictures would come out. She knew that Maria would never notice her car in its parking spot. Nor would expect that Adam would follow her example and engage an investigator, even one who wasn't official. There was probably nothing more to be achieved that evening and Sally was weary and starving.

She collected a pizza on her way back to the hotel and ate it hungrily. Somehow, she needed to be back at Maria's apartment early the next morning to catch her and the man leaving. If she could get a picture of them, together with the picture she had of Brad and the au pair, it ought to be good ammunition for a counter claim that the child was not being looked after by the mother who claimed she wanted custody.

Sally wasn't sure how it might work in this country but surely, it was logical that the child should be with the parent able to spend the most time with him. If there was any argument about herself and Adam, surely Maria's man friend would make her equally unsuitable?

After a restless night, Sally drove across town once more. She stopped at the apartment block and sat with her camera ready. The silver car was missing and though she waited for some time, there was no movement. Other people came out of the building and drove away. Brad and the au pair arrived, Brad once more looking angry and defiant. To her shock, he detached himself from the au pair and ran over to Sally's car.

'I knew you'd come to rescue me,' he yelled through the window. 'Please let me come home with you, Sally. Please . . . I hate it here. There's nothing to do . . . and Ingrid doesn't like me . . . and I hate Uncle Ted and my mummy doesn't really want me . . . and . . . and . . .'

'Brad, please. I haven't come to take you home. I er . . . I called to see your mummy.'

'She isn't there. They came back late last night and had to go to work early today. Ingrid's taking me to that horrible school again.' Tears were streaming down his cheeks and Sally felt she would like to snatch him away and take him back to Adam.

Ingrid arrived beside her car and began to shout at the child. She hammered on the door and told Sally to go away before she called the police.

'I came to see Mrs Edwards. To plead with her to let Brad go home to his father.'

'She's not here. She's busy all day and all evening. Now go away and leave us alone. I've got to get him to school and I have to meet someone.'

'I bet you have. You'll be hearing more from us.'

'Now go away or I call police.'

'Don't go Sally,' sobbed Brad. 'Please rescue me. I hate living in this place.'

'I'll try to help, darling. Please be good now and I'll see what I can do.'

She could do nothing more without getting herself arrested and she drove away leaving Brad screaming and hitting out at the au pair. She sobbed as she drove, wondering if there was anything she could do to remain within the law. She needed one more photograph, a conclusive picture of Maria and her lover. Somehow, she needed to occupy herself and try to organise some appointments for work for the next few hours.

It was hard to concentrate, but she managed to contact a couple more clients and be back outside the apartment by early evening. The silver car was already parked in its spot and she cursed silently. She was on the point of driving away when Maria and her friend came out of the door. They were dressed up, clearly going out for the evening.

She raised the camera and took her picture. Suddenly, Maria turned and came towards her. She looked angry and in a panic, Sally started her car and drove past her and out of the car park. She saw Maria running to their own car and they were following.

Her heart sinking, Sally drove as fast as she dared in the unfamiliar streets, trying to shake them off. She saw a sign to the motorway and turned towards it. It would be foolish indeed to try and outrun the sports car and once she saw him get into the outside lane, ready to drive past her and on to the fast road, she turned away and despite the hooting of horns behind her, went back into the quieter suburban road.

There was no way that he could cross the traffic to follow her. By the time he left at the next exit, she would be miles away. Laughing in almost hysterical relief, she drove back to her hotel. She needed to get the pictures to Adam as soon as possible and away from the city. There was still someone in reception, so she paid her bill and was ready to make a very early start the next day. She forgot about her intended holiday trip. Brad needed to be back home as soon as possible.

The morning traffic was heavy and she took some time to be clear of it. She felt a sense of relief to be on the road back towards her quieter life. She was in the office soon after midday and dialled Adam's number.

'Hi, it's Sally. I've got some pictures I think you might like to see.'

'What are you talking about? Where are you? I've just had a call from Maria. Something about you spying on her? She was furious and saying I'll regret sending you to blackmail her. What on earth have you done?'

'I'm sorry if I made things difficult.

But I've got proof that she has someone living with her . . . well, staying at her apartment sometimes. And she's spending hardly any time with Brad. There's some au pair who takes him to school and . . .'

'Whoa. Slow down. I'm coming over. Where are you?'

'The office. I'll wait here.' She was shaking and made herself a strong cup of coffee. She realised she'd missed breakfast but didn't want to leave in case Adam arrived.

She saw his car stop and felt her heart give a lurch as he got out and came towards the door. It was all she could do to stop herself from rushing into his arms. She so needed a hug.

'Come on, you crazy woman. Tell me what on earth you've been doing?'

She explained about her trip and plugged the camera into her computer. They looked at the pictures together and Adam punched his fist into his other hand when he saw Brad looking so upset.

'How dare she? How dare she complain about me? The woman's deranged. I've got to get him back. Away from her. I won't have him used this way.'

'I hope I haven't made anything worse. It would have been fine if Brad hadn't spotted me. They'd never have known I was even in the area.'

'Never mind. You did well. I'll get these right off to my solicitor. Can I use your machine? I'll e-mail them to him.'

'This technology is amazing, isn't it? Fancy being able to take a picture and send it anywhere you want, in seconds.' Adam called his solicitor and told him to expect the pictures. He talked for a few minutes and then turned to Sally.

'Would you be willing to make a statement?' She nodded. 'That's fine then. Tomorrow morning? See you then. Hope that's OK? Ten tomorrow morning.'

'Oh, Adam, I felt so helpless seeing him like that. He was so upset and so angry. Kept talking about being rescued. I was half expecting him to start an asthma attack he was so distressed.'

'You do love me, don't you?' he asked suddenly.

'Of course I do, Adam. I'd hardly be going through all this if I didn't.'

'And you will marry me, once it's all sorted?'

'Yes please,' she whispered as he took her in his arms. He held her close for a moment.

'Not quite what I intended as a proposal, but you gave me the answer I hoped for. I'll pick you up at nine-thirty. And thank you. Thank you so much.'

When he arrived the next day, he looked very pale and his mouth was set in a grim line.

'I'm afraid Maria's got in with a counter claim. The solicitor rang first thing. It seems she's claiming to be very upset by your visit and has charged me with sending my mistress . . . no, don't say anything . . . to spy on her. She's accusing me of trying to upset her and her son by allowing Brad to see you deliberately. You were trying to break down the stability she is able to give him.'

'But that's poppycock. The poor child is in a dreadful state and he's being looked after by some girl who wants only to dump him at school so she can spend the day with her own boyfriend. And Maria hardly spent any time with Brad. She was back late at night and the next night she did come back early, she went out again in less than an hour. And she has the revolting Uncle Ted living in most of the time.'

'So you did do a thorough spying job on her?' Adam laughed. 'Knew her every move for a couple of days. And I thought you'd gone to AKL to work.'

'I did. I was planning a little holiday up to Northland, but I sort of had to forget that.'

'When everything's sorted, we'll go there together. It's wonderful.'

'Hadn't we better get this over with?

How much do I say to the solicitor without proving that Maria was right? I was spying on her.'

'We'll tell him everything and he can decide what to use. It may look as if it's gone a bit pear-shaped at the moment but I do appreciate what you were trying to achieve.'

It was a difficult interview and Adam's solicitor was somewhat disapproving of her actions.

'It might have been more useful if you had engaged a private investigator,' Mr Bailey told her. 'But, we do have the pictures and may manage without revealing their source. The confrontation with Brad might present more of a problem, but we'll see what we can do.'

'But he was begging me to rescue him. To rescue him. As if he was being held against his will. Surely that can't be right? And Maria was spending hardly any time with him. She doesn't want him. She wants a weapon to use against his father. And the anonymous letters must prove she's unstable.'

Mr Bailey's eyes gleamed.

'What anonymous letters?' he demanded.

'We don't know for sure that she sent them. Forget about them,' Adam insisted. Sally shrugged.

By the time they left the solicitor's office, she felt drained. They had a quick lunch together before Adam rushed off to do a couple of jobs. Sally sat in her office wondering what on earth she had got herself into.

Her phone rang at seven o'clock the next morning.

'Sally? I have to go to Auckland. Brad's in hospital. It's the usual, but Maria's blaming it all on me . . . well you, actually. You caused him to be stressed, evidently. She says I must go and sort it out but really, it's Brad demanding to see me. He says I know what to do and she knows nothing. Needless to say, it's not making anything easier.'

'I'm coming with you to Auckland. If I really did cause all this, it's up to me to help sort it out. Pick me up. I'll be ready by the time you get here.'

She showered in record time and flung on some clothes. She swigged a quick mouthful of coffee and grabbed a slightly black banana from the fruit bowl. She saw Adam's car arrive and rushed out of the apartment to meet him.

'I'm getting used to this road,' she remarked. 'Doesn't seem five minutes since I was driving the opposite direction.'

It was mid morning when Adam's car stopped in the hospital car park. 'I'll sit in the coffee place, if there is one. I don't want to risk meeting Maria and causing any more stress. Come and tell me how Brad's doing, won't you?' Sally asked.

'Of course. If you're sure. It might be best until I see what's going on.'

She made two cups of coffee last for two hours. At last, Adam arrived looking weary. Brad was demanding to see Sally, once he knew she was nearby. Immediately, she leapt up, longing to see the little boy.

'So, how he is?' she asked anxiously as they hurried along the corridors.

'Not too bad now. It's the usual thing. Nebuliser and increased oxygen for a while. He's almost ready to be discharged, but even that is a problem. Officially, he is still required to stay with Maria, but he gets mildly hysterical when I suggest it.'

'Sally, you came to rescue me. I knew you would.' He held out his arms to her and she hugged him.

'What are you doing in here, you old silly?'

'Better than being at Maria's. It's horrible there. And Ingrid doesn't know about children or anything. I want to come home with you.'

'We'll see,' Sally said with an anxious look at his father.

'Oh how delightfully cosy,' said a new voice. Sally swung round and came face to face with Maria. 'Couldn't even come and see your own son without dragging your . . . your trollop along.'

'What's a trollop?' asked Brad with great interest.

'Someone who's no good,' Maria snapped. 'I see you're feeling better this morning.'

Adam's face was white and he was boiling with anger.

'How dare you? Calling Sally names is serving no useful purpose and it's upsetting Brad.'

'He looks all right to me,' Maria snapped.

Sally let go of Brad's hand and rose, ready to leave them to it.

'Don't go, Sally. I want you here and I want to come back home with you and Daddy.'

Maria exploded and the air was filled with angry remarks and the sort of remarks no child should have to hear. Brad began to sob and soon the ward sister arrived.

'I cannot have this noise and you're upsetting your son as well as other patients. Leave. now, please.'

Sheepishly, they trooped out, leaving

the sister to calm Brad.

The battle raged on for several minutes and Sally felt desperate to get away. She couldn't bear it any longer.

'You are discussing the life of a human being, here. A little boy. Your own son. He isn't some object to be fought over and used as a bargaining tool. For goodness sake, stop behaving like a pair of spoilt children fighting over a toy. Surely, Brad is old enough to make his own choices. It seems to me that you are too busy to give him the time he needs, Maria. You sent for Adam the minute things got tough. Now, sort yourselves out and I'll wait in the car.'

'How dare you interfere? You're right. He is our son and we'll make the decisions for him. I shall be spending more time with him in future. Things have changed here.'

'Have you lost your job?' Adam asked. Maria went white.

'You can pay me an allowance and pay for Brad's expenses too. Least you can do. You can't expect me to pay for your son on my own.'

'But you're not on your own, are you? According to Brad, Uncle Ted is staying with you.'

'That's my business.'

'I'm not sure it is. Maybe we should ask Brad what he wants,' Adam said thoughtfully.

'You know very well what he'll say. You and that woman have brainwashed him.'

'In that case, we'll get an independent opinion. I'm sure you know someone in the psychiatry department. We'll get someone to talk with him and see what he wants. But I'll warn you, Maria, if you do have custody of him, you will look after him properly. Yourself, and not some au pair. And if you object so much to me having a new partner, then I trust you will do the same. No-one but Brad in your life.'

Two pink spots appeared on Maria's cheeks and she was about to launch into a new speech when Sally returned and asked Adam for his car keys.

'We're going to ask Brad what he wants to do,' Adam announced.

'That sounds like the best plan,' Sally said quietly. Adam caught her hand and gave it a squeeze.

'We'll go and ask him together, Maria. You can do the talking, but if you say anything to try and prejudice his answers, then I shall call my solicitor again.'

Maria nodded and mother and father went into the ward again. The sister hovered close by, unwilling to allow a repeat of their previous behaviour. Nervously, Sally waited outside the door, peering in through the glass to see if she could judge the outcome. She did not need to ask when she saw Adam's grin.

'I won't be seeing you again,' Maria snapped at Sally. 'I shall want to see Brad occasionally, but I won't cause any more trouble. You win. Besides, I'm not really the maternal type. I plan to get another job soon. Ted will help me.'

She swept away along the corridor and hopefully, out of their lives.

'She's agreed to the divorce as soon as it can be arranged and promises not to contest the custody,' Adam said happily.

'That's wonderful, Adam. So we have a future together after all.'

'No regrets?'

'None at all. My parents may grumble a bit, but they'll come round.'

They stayed in Auckland for the night and were able to take Brad home the next day. They sang silly songs all the way back and the car was filled with chatter and the sound of a little boy who had the future he wanted.

There was a message from Rob waiting for her at the apartment. She called him back.

'What is it, Rob?' she asked cautiously.

'I wanted to be the first to tell you my news. I'm getting married.'

'Wow. That was quick.'

'I know. But sometimes, you know

immediately when something's right. It was like that with Bronwyn. I, well, I met your mother the other day and told her. She took it quite well. I wanted to tell you before she did.'

'I wish you happiness, Rob. Really I do. Actually, things are getting sorted for me too. Adam and I are going to marry as soon as his divorce is settled.'

'That's great news. I'm pleased for you. Actually, I hinted to your mother that you may be staying in New Zealand.'

'Rob, how could you? What did she say?'

'I think she was expecting it. Made some comment about it only being a day away.'

'It is. I wish you happiness, Rob. Truly I do.'

'And you, Sally. Be happy.'

'I intend to be.' She hung up and smiled.

We do hope that you have enjoyed reading this large print book.

Did you know that all of our titles are available for purchase?

We publish a wide range of high quality large print books including:
Romances, Mysteries, Classics
General Fiction
Non Fiction and Westerns

Special interest titles available in large print are:
The Little Oxford Dictionary
Music Book, Song Book
Hymn Book, Service Book

Also available from us courtesy of Oxford University Press:
Young Readers' Dictionary
(large print edition)
Young Readers' Thesaurus
(large print edition)

For further information or a free brochure, please contact us at:
Ulverscroft Large Print Books Ltd.,
The Green, Bradgate Road, Anstey,
Leicester, LE7 7FU, England.
Tel: (00 44) **0116 236 4325**
Fax: (00 44) **0116 234 0205**

NEVER LET ME GO

Toni Anders

It was love at first sight for Nurse Chloe Perle and ambitious Dr. Adam Raven, but their employer had plans for his daughter, Susannah, and the young doctor. When Adam informed Chloe his career would always come before romantic entanglements, she left the practice for a position far away in the Cotswolds. There, she attracted the attention of Benedict, a handsome young artist. Afraid that he had lost Chloe forever, Adam begged her friend, Betty, the only person who knew her whereabouts, to help him.

AZETTE FROM JERSEY

Irene Castle

When Azette flew from Jersey to the West Country, to find her favourite cousin Dennis, she also made new friends: Jane, now her flat-mate, and Mandy, who refuses to name her baby's father and needs help. At Jane's family home Azette is introduced to Andrew, a handsome — if moody — farmer . . . She is reunited with her cousin Dennis, but suddenly their relationship changes, and their plans to return to Jersey together crumble. Now Azette has a difficult decision to make . . .